To Kyle and with best wishes
Tony Hayter
November 2011

# *HALCYON FURY*

## R. ANTON HOUGH

All rights reserved. No part of this book shall be reproduced or transmitted in any form or by any means, electronic, mechanical, magnetic, photographic including photocopying, recording or by any information storage and retrieval system, without prior written permission of the publisher. No patent liability is assumed with respect to the use of the information contained herein. Although every precaution has been taken in the preparation of this book, the publisher and author assume no responsibility for errors or omissions. Neither is any liability assumed for damages resulting from the use of the information contained herein.

Copyright © 2011 by R. Anton Hough
Cover photograph by R. Stephen Schneider
Author photograph by Victoria Brueckmann Hough

ISBN 0-7414-6558-2

Printed in the United States of America

This is a work of fiction. Names, characters, places, and incidents either are the product of the author's imagination or are used fictitiously. Any resemblance to actual events or locales or persons, living or dead, is entirely coincidental.

Published May 2011

INFINITY PUBLISHING
1094 New DeHaven Street, Suite 100
West Conshohocken, PA 19428-2713
Toll-free (877) BUY BOOK
Local Phone (610) 941-9999
Fax (610) 941-9959
Info@buybooksontheweb.com
www.buybooksontheweb.com

To the memory of my grandfather
Dr. Anton J. Carlson
Professor of Physiology
who taught me how to fish
and was my earliest mentor in the
life sciences

and

To the memory of my father
Dr. Jack L. Hough
Professor of Geology and Oceanography
who taught me how to sail
and was my earliest mentor in the
freshwater and marine sciences

# Prologue

Wet footprints trailed behind a pair of barefoot joggers on the firm sand at the water's edge along the bay front of Traverse City. It was nine a.m. on Monday, August 2, and young professionals were getting their lattes-to-go at the coffee shops on Front Street. Tourist boutiques were opening their doors to another quiet, pleasant day in vacationland.

It was quiet as well in a second floor courtroom on Washington Street, but it was anything but pleasant for Paul Tyson, who was sitting at the defense table waiting for the bailiff to announce the State of Michigan's case against him. Dressed in a blue blazer and slacks, Paul was motionless except for his right heel which tapped a light rapid rhythm on the floor. Beside Paul were his attorneys, Craig Basham and Harold Holmes, both in gray suits.

The prosecutor and his assistant were seated calmly at their table in their black pinstripes. In the audience behind the prosecutor's table sat the family of Paul's alleged victim, Ronald Withers. The bailiff announced the case, and the judge called the prosecutor and defense attorney Basham to the bench. The prosecutor spoke to Basham in a low voice.

"Has your client changed his mind about our plea bargain offer?"

"Not a chance," replied Basham.

The judge sent them back to their tables and directed the bailiff to call in the first group from the prospective jury pool downstairs. He asked the spectators to move to the rear of the gallery so that the prospective jurors could occupy the first few rows of seats. The twenty-four citizens filed in and took their seats. The judge thanked them for being present and willing to serve, explained the jury selection process, and outlined the case. Using a randomized list, the bailiff called fourteen people by the numbers they had been assigned in the jury pool room downstairs and directed them to be seated in the jury box in the order they were called. The judge began the voir dire process.

"Number seven, please state your name and occupation."

"Douglas Hird, septic service operator."

Craig Basham rose. "Mr. Hird, before today, were you aware of this case involving graduate students Paul Tyson and Ronald Withers at the Rynar University Limnology Institute?"

"No, sir, I was not."

"Do you know anyone at the institute?"

"No."

"No further questions, your honor." Craig Basham sat down.

The prosecutor rose. "Mr. Hird, do you have any relatives or friends who work in law enforcement?"

"No."

"Thank you. No further questions." Mr. Hird was allowed to remain in his seat in the jury box.

Number ten was called to the stand, and the Judge asked his name and occupation.

"Fritz Rehring, retired business executive."

Craig asked if he had heard about the case.

"Yes, I have read about it in the paper."

"Do you have any strong feelings one way or the other about the events of June twelfth involving the injury of Ronald Withers on the research ship *Halcyon*, or about the defendant?"

"No, I do not."

"Do you know anyone at the university?"

"I know the dean of the business school."

"Will you be able to listen objectively to the evidence presented, and render a fair and impartial judgment?"

"Yes I will."

Craig had no further questions.

The prosecutor asked the man if he had any connection with law enforcement. He did not. Mr. Rehring kept his seat, and the judge moved on.

Number seventeen was questioned next.

"Tamika White. I'm a nurse."

The judge himself asked Ms. White the obvious question. "Do you work at the hospital?" She did.

"Were you familiar with patient Ronald Withers?"

"Yes, I treated him in the emergency room."

"Ms. White, the court thanks you and excuses you." It was clear to the judge that she was too close to the case. She rose and left the courtroom, and the bailiff called another prospective juror from the gallery to take the vacated seat in the jury box.

Number twenty, Marilyn Frey, was a housewife. She had not heard about the case, knew no one at the institute and had no connection with law enforcement. Both defense and prosecution moved on.

Number fourteen was a vintner on Mission Point named Aaron Artis, who knew about the case, but only generally, and indicated that he could be impartial. He also knew no one at the institute nor in law enforcement, and he too was allowed to keep his seat.

Next came number one, Robert Jacobson.

"I'm a high school science teacher."

"Do you know about this case?" asked Craig Basham.

"Yes, I have read about it."

"Do you know anyone at the institute?"

"Not personally, but I have taken my classes to visit there many times."

"Can you be impartial in this case?"

"Sure."

"No further questions."

The prosecutor rose. "Your honor, I wish to thank and excuse Mr. Jacobson." The prosecutor was quick to use one of his allotted peremptory challenges. He did not want this man to be anywhere near the jury. Educated in science, the man was probably too intelligent and objective to be dazzled easily by the prosecutor's courtroom tactics and too likely to raise doubts in the jury room. His seat was taken by another from the gallery.

Number three, June Bailey, and number twenty-four, Barbara Bonner, were both housewives who knew nothing about the case and knew no one at the institute. Ms. Bonner had a cousin who was a loss prevention detective in retail, but neither prosecution nor defense thought that this was a significant problem. Both women remained in the jury box.

As the voir dire droned on, defendant Paul Tyson's eyes lost focus, the voices in the courtroom became muffled and far away, and Paul lapsed into a memory of the past several weeks since that morning when his pleasant, productive world as a graduate student had been shattered by the simple act of opening the pages of a new issue of a scientific journal. It had begun exactly two months ago on the afternoon of Wednesday, June 2.

# Chapter

## 1

"We're in a world of trouble," muttered Paul Tyson as his red '66 Mustang GT screamed into a power slide coming out of the last turn on U.S. 31 North approaching Elk Rapids. From the passenger seat, Joan Brockton saw three deer standing freeze-framed in the road and staring toward the car as it hurtled at them.

"Jesus…" she managed to gasp just as the edge of the right rear bumper took out one of the animals before it could jump clear.

Paul had steered into the slide, choosing to hit one of the deer rather than spin out into the trees along the roadside. He skidded the car to a stop on the sandy shoulder, and he and Joan walked fifty yards back to the deer lying in the grass next to a line of poplar trees. The settling dust glowed in the late afternoon sun as they stood and watched the life fade from the small buck's eyes like dying embers. Paul gazed silently until Joan crossed her arms and turned to him.

"Okay Paul, before you kill the rest of the deer in northern Michigan, please tell me what's going on? I've never seen you worked up like this."

"I'll show you," Paul answered. He turned back toward the car, and Joan followed. As they got in, he grabbed the June issue of the *Journal of Freshwater and Oceanic Sciences* from the backseat and dropped it in her lap. "This arrived today. Look on page 527."

She picked up the journal and thumbed to that page. "This is an article by Ron Withers and his doctoral advisor, Dr. Bates. They're part of the limnology group here at the Institute. What's the problem?"

"At least a third of it is my data."

Joan stared at the article. "You can't be serious."

"Positive. These graphs are right out of my computer files. No one else here has done experiments like that, and as far as I know, I'm the only one here who uses that particular type of graphics. I know my data."

Joan sat in silence as Paul drove the rest of the way to Elk Rapids. As he pulled on to River Street and drove past the bright red geranium planters along the row of shops, galleries and restaurants, she asked, "Why would Withers and Bates do this?"

"Bates is having trouble getting his grant renewed, and Withers has been striking out with a lot of his own experiments. If Bates doesn't get his renewal, he probably won't get tenure, and Ron won't get his PhD. My guess is, it's Ron's attempt to rescue them both. I'm not sure Bates knows he did it."

"How could he hope to get away with it?"

"Well, for one thing, my raw data books are missing, so it will be hard for me to document that it is my work."

Paul turned down toward the harbor and glanced over at the white frame library that looks out over the bay from a high grassy grove of pine and birch; it was as though a small corner of Martha's Vineyard had been carved out and nestled here along the blue panorama of Grand Traverse Bay. In the harbor the boats were all nodding gently in their slips like sleepy horses in their stalls. Paul parked the Mustang in front of his boat, and he and Joan walked out onto his finger dock and stepped aboard. The only people they saw on the docks were an elderly man pushing a cart of groceries, trailed by his wife with a small dog on a leash. The old couple carefully boarded their small sailboat. Gulls circled and bleated overhead as Paul went below to get a couple of cold beers.

Paul Tyson was a thirty-three year old doctoral student studying plankton ecology under the direction of Dr. Walter Perry at the Rynar University Limnology Institute in Traverse City, Michigan. The university had been built early in the 20$^{th}$ century with timber money on the Rynar Estate property at the foot of Grand Traverse Bay in the heart of one of the most beautiful areas of the northern Great Lakes. The university had enjoyed rapid growth in the 1980s. With the help of several major federal grants, the Institute, known locally by the acronym "RULI", had been established to study Lake Michigan limnology, better known as freshwater ecology. After acquiring a 35-foot Maine lobsterman for short range work, and a 115-foot converted minesweeper for longer Great Lakes cruises, the president of the university had been able to attract prominent limnologist Dr. Karen Tollefson from Lund, Sweden, to direct the Institute.

Paul had been at RULI for nearly four years, and was about to start writing his doctoral dissertation. He lived on a slightly aging black 41-foot center-cockpit ketch that he had inherited after having crewed for a number of years for its famed owner, the writer Ian Kerrigan. The old man, in failing health with no family of his own, had grown to appreciate and depend on Paul's good-natured competence and loyalty, and regarded him as the son he never had. Paul kept *Tondeleyo* at the same slip she had always occupied along the sea wall in the Elk Rapids marina, where the blue-green water from Elk Lake flows through the old power dam into Traverse Bay. Kerrigan had left a modest trust to pay for the annual slip fee. It was a perfect arrangement for a graduate student with no income other than the slave wages of graduate assistantships, and Paul was grateful, though he was slightly embarrassed by this good fortune. The boat was roomy enough for one or two people to live aboard comfortably, although as on most sailboats the shower was small, and like most boaters Paul used the marina shower most of the time. Paul lived on *Tondeleyo* year around. In the winter, air bubblers at the bottom of his slip kept the ice away from the hull, and electric heaters kept the cabin cozy.

Twenty-eight year old Joan Brockton was a fellow graduate student at the Institute. Paul had gotten to know her at the weekly grad student association seminars. As an evolutionary biologist using state-of-the-art molecular gene techniques, Joan sometimes needled Paul about his more traditional environmental biology and its lack of genetic approach. Paul took it good naturedly, and lately their friendship had grown to something more than a mutual interest in aquatic science. They had similar backgrounds, both growing up in big city suburbs and attending urban universities. Joan was a graduate of Wayne State University in Detroit, and Paul's *alma mater* was Northwestern University in Evanston, Illinois. Paul was tempted to pretend Chicago chauvinism and tease her about Detroit, but he refrained from that because he knew that not all of Detroit's bad press was deserved.

As they sat in the cockpit of *Tondeleyo*, watching the last traces of the sunlight glowing from behind the Old Mission point that separated the two arms of Traverse Bay, Joan leaned against the stern rail and idly sipped her Corona.

Paul relaxed watching the June breezes swirl through her honey-brown hair like bank swallows among the dock lines. But the pleasant interlude was interrupted by her quiet but unavoidable question.

"What are you going to do?"

He knocked back a swallow of his beer, and ran his fingers through his coarse brown hair and down along the scar on his jaw line while he focused his hazel eyes on his boat shoes.

"Don't know. I need to talk to Dr. Perry. He's in Washington right now, but I'll see him at ASFOS in Ann Arbor next week."

Paul was talking about the annual meeting of the American Society of Freshwater and Oceanic Sciences, at which he was scheduled to present a paper.

"Withers and Bates will be there too, of course. Where it will go from there, I have no clue right now."

"Why is Bates having trouble getting his grant renewed?" asked Joan. "He's pretty good, isn't he?"

Paul shrugged and said, "Yeah, he's a good scientist, but he's got two problems a lot of academic ecologists have. Number one, the folks in molecular biology have been getting fatter and fatter shares of the dwindling federal research money, and environmental scientists are fighting over the scraps that are left. Number two, a lot of Bates' work requires relatively long-term study, and the rate of publication is intrinsically slower than the agency panels like to see. Add to that the bad luck of having a couple of particularly slow grad students in his lab, and bingo he's in trouble."

"Well," she grinned, "Didn't I tell you that you ecologists should get into real science like I am?"

He gave her a playful swat on the butt as she swiveled away and clambered through the hatch down to the salon. Paul grinned, drained his beer and followed her below.

# Chapter 2

The next morning, as Thursday, June 3, dawned to a pale cloudless sky, Paul and Joan sleepily drank orange juice in the cool, dew-laden cockpit. They wore their usual khaki cargo shorts, but had pulled on sweatshirts in the cool air. With his RULI ball cap pulled low to block the morning glare, Paul watched a small perch rise through the translucent water and toy with a foam bubble drifting on the placid surface. Then yesterday's discovery flooded back to mind.

"First thing I'm doing today is getting my latest data off the hard drive of the lab computer and hope to hell Withers hasn't gotten that yet. My new raw data book is locked up here on the boat, fortunately. Then I guess I'll review my PowerPoint slides and run through my Ann Arbor talk a few times."

They buttoned up *Tondeleyo*, got in the Mustang, and headed back south on US 31 toward Traverse City and the institute. Passing the place where they had hit the deer, they noticed that the DNR had already removed the carcass.

"Poor thing," said Joan.

They drove on in silence past the cherry orchards, meadows, and stands of beech, maple and evergreens, followed by the shopping strips of the village of Acme, and finally the bright blue foot of the East Arm of Traverse Bay lined with fudge shops, woolen goods stores, amusement parks, and waterfront resorts approaching the city center.

Reaching the institute on the West Arm, they squinted at the shimmering surface of the harbor water as they drove into the parking lot. The 115-foot *Halcyon* was at her mooring, her dark blue hull and white superstructure gleaming in the sun. A couple of deck hands were hosing down the foredeck. Her twin cargo masts, bristling with radio and meteorology hardware, drew lazy circles in the sky as she gently moved to the swell entering the small harbor. Paul stopped the car and stared past the *Halcyon* at the bay for a moment. "I love these lakes, but science has lost a lot of its luster since I saw the article yesterday."

"I don't blame you," said Joan. "Paul, I'm sorry for my crack about 'real science' last night. I didn't really mean it." She kissed him and got out of the car. "I'll be up to here in experiments for a while; I've got some difficult gene probes to make. If I don't see you in the next few days, good luck in Ann Arbor."

"Thanks, Joan." Paul's eyes followed her athletic body moving easily as she walked over to her Blazer to get her briefcase. Small breasted and trim hipped, she was not a Playboy beauty – but to him she was more alluring than those hyper-siliconed cover girls. She turned and shot one last smile at him on her way to the biology building.

Paul went into the limnology building to Dr. Perry's lab, where he had worked for over three years generating some excellent data on the effects of global warming on phytoplankton algae in northern Lake Michigan. It was Paul's data on the population sizes and diversity of these algae that Ron Withers had stolen to support his own work on zooplankton ecology in the same areas.

Paul was halfway through the job of making a second backup of his new data onto two duplicate flash dives and deleting the hard drive files, when in the corner of his eye he noticed someone at the door staring at him. He turned to see Ron Withers quickly moving off down the hall. Paul froze like a cat watching a bird in the grass, fighting back the urge to chase him down. *Looking for more of my data, you bastard? I thought we were colleagues, for Christ sake.*

Just then *Halcyon's* chief engineer, Chuck Jordan, ducked his head in the doorway. "Tyson! What the hell ghost did you just see? You look like the morning after we left Manitowoc last summer. Hungover as I've ever seen anybody."

"Hey Chief. No ghosts and no hangover, but things aren't going real well right now. I wish it was just Manitowoc boilermakers, but I'll deal with it. What's up?"

"We're getting *Halcyon* ready for the Mackinac Straits run. When's your next cruise?"

"I go to sea a week from Saturday, after the ASFOS meeting in Ann Arbor."

"Well, you better get your shit together by then. You know old Rubba-dub likes a happy ship." The chief clattered on down the hall in his noisy knee brace toward the marine operations office.

*Rubba-dub. Captain Rubba-dub.* "*Rubba-dub-dub, three men in a tub...*" Paul smiled briefly at the nursery rhyme nickname some people used for *Halcyon's* skipper, Antonio Robado. Few uttered it in Robado's presence, despite the fact that it was used with fondness and respect for the short but powerfully built and highly experienced captain.

But Paul's smile faded as he realized that Ron Withers was scheduled to be on Paul's *Halcyon* cruise coming up, and worse yet, Ron's mentor Dr. Eldon Bates would be chief scientist on the cruise.

Paul finished up a few odds and ends in the lab, and closed down his operation for the time he would be away in Ann Arbor. Pocketing the duplicate flash drives containing his slide show document, he went back to his Mustang and drove out of the parking lot back toward Elk Rapids.

Pulling into the harbor lot, Paul went aboard *Tondeleyo* and began preparing for his trip to the Ann Arbor meeting. He spent a couple of hours making final edits on the slides he wanted to use. Paul had become adept with the PowerPoint program. He ignored the frustrating and confining template formats and delighted in creating stunning slides with his own style. The background for all the figures and tables was a marine blue that graded from pale at the top to dark at the bottom as though you were seeing the data underwater. He scrupulously avoided using large data-dense tables that were impossible to read in a seminar room. He couldn't believe how many people still did that at meetings.

Paul rehearsed his talk until he was confident that he could deliver a presentation that Dr. Perry would be proud of. A recent recipient of the Tyler Prize for Environmental Achievement at the White House, Perry was well known and respected, and that was a powerful incentive for his students to live up to the reputation of the Perry lab.

On Friday Paul tried to relax with some overdue boat chores. *Tondeleyo's* fuel line needed to be cleaned and the filter replaced, which were messy jobs that occupied him for most of the morning. In the afternoon he turned his attention to the aging davit lines that hoisted the dinghy. He cut some lengths of new Dacron line and spliced them onto the brass fittings, a pleasant task that wore away half of the warm afternoon. He finished the day replacing the caulking around the base of the dorade vents on the foredeck. It had become cracked and discolored, and soon would not be watertight.

For an early dinner Paul strolled over across U.S. 31 to a riverfront restaurant for a beer and burger on their patio. A young guitar player was doing a passable job of covering Jimmy Buffett songs, and the guy sang a few of his own tunes that weren't half bad. Several patrons had come to the restaurant's docks in their boats from summer cottages on Elk Lake, and those folks were singing along more loudly as the beer flowed. But without Joan to share the evening with him, Paul soon returned to *Tondeleyo* and read some of a paperback sea story in his bunk before turning off the cabin lights.

On Saturday, Paul packed a small sea bag with the few clothes he would need in Ann Arbor, and spent the rest of the day up in the Island House library on the hill. As he had done many times before, he amassed a shopping bag full of used paperback novels that were perpetually on sale in the basement for twenty-five cents apiece. When he finished them he would give them back to the library to sell again. Out on a bench in front of the library, he enjoyed the view of the bay for a while. But his view kept getting clouded by the thought of the quickly approaching meeting, where he was certain to cross paths with Ron Withers again. He shuddered, thinking of how Dr. Perry would react to the news about the data.

After a quick dinner of warmed up canned food aboard *Tondeleyo,* Paul gave Joan a call.

"I'm pretty much ready. But I feel like a gladiator about to enter the Coliseum without a weapon."

"Stay cool. You'll be fine."

"Thanks. I'll miss you down there."

"Me too you. Bye Paul."

## CHAPTER 3

Late Sunday morning Paul was on southbound I-75 below Grayling on his way to Ann Arbor. In no hurry, Paul dawdled along at about sixty in the slow lane, enjoying the sound of the well-tuned old 289 V8 burbling through the twin tailpipes in the hazy afternoon. The Mustang coupe had the original white GT side-stripe below the doors, and the candy-apple red finish was in mint condition.

He drove below the speed limit, not so much to avoid a ticket as to keep his carbon emission footprint from being worse than it already was without using all four barrels of the carburetor. But southbound weekend warrior traffic was already building, and the congestion was slowing everyone down anyway. Normally he would avoid Sunday for this trip, but he wanted to get to Ann Arbor in time for the Sunday evening mixer at the meeting; it would be the fastest way to find Dr. Perry and deliver the bombshell news.

Here on the road he had been daydreaming about Joan, when out of nowhere a high-riding sport pickup roared by him and cut him off, nearly leaving the pavement as it swerved in around a car in the left lane that wasn't doing the usual 85. "GO AHEAD AND FLIP IT IN THE DITCH, YOU ASSHOLES. HELL ISN'T HALF FULL!" Paul barked out the window at the cocky twenty-somethings as though they could hear him, his blood pressure spiking 200.

Wondering when he had ever been as angry as he was now over Ron's plagiarism, a memory search took him back to his high school football days in suburban Chicago, and the incident that had added the permanent scar along the angular jaw of his strong-featured face.

Paul had been five-eleven and one hundred sixty pounds, the same as now. "Just the right size for a defensive back," the coach had said. Paul was tough, but he was not quite fast enough to be a starter, and he mostly played on the special teams. On the opening kickoff of the last game of his junior year, he broke the kick returner's leg with a clean but jarring tackle. On the next kickoff, an opposing player retaliated with a blindside elbow to Paul's jaw. "You little shit," Paul seethed as he tore the kid's helmet off and grabbed him in a choke hold that could have killed the kid if his teammates hadn't pulled him away. Paul ended up with a game ejection and six stitches in his jaw.

In college he had been in a few minor scuffles in intramural touch football, and one brief argument with a roommate over a girl, but no major temper problems that he could think of. He remembered always being a little restless as a youth and wishing he could have been a frontiersman or explorer along the lines of Lewis and Clark, but he never saw himself as a warrior type. While majoring in biology at Northwestern he did become excited by the potential for a career of field research in environmental science, and striving then for grad school, he was able to finish his B.S. cum laude.

Paul's thoughts returned to Joan as he drove. Their intensifying friendship was vying pleasantly with his research for prominence in his life. He was drawn to her muscular body, honed by soccer in high school, varsity softball while a chemistry major in college, and frequent running ever since.

But especially attractive to him was Joan's combination of gentle attentiveness and confident scientific intuition. Her superb seminar to the grad group last fall on Coho salmon physiology had blown everyone away. Paul had never seen a first-year grad student with her level of maturity and independent thinking. Most were hardly able to formulate their own questions, hypotheses and experimental designs. Joan was doing that right out of the gate, and was proposing to use methods with novel combinations of the latest biotechnology. She was going to go far very quickly. *Damn shame she couldn't come down with me this week, but what the hell – I need to concentrate on this Withers situation without dragging her all though it.*

A few miles on, the usual spate of orange highway construction barrels brought a stretch of I-75 down to one lane, and traffic slowed to a stop-and-go crawl. Of course it was just beyond a rest area that Paul had passed up, and before long he had to pee like a race horse.

A half hour of crawling along brought him to the satisfying sight of those idiots in the truck that had cut him off, sitting on the shoulder watching their radiator blowing steam. Sometimes there is justice. Soon traffic picked up and Paul got to the next rest area before bursting his bladder.

Two and a half hours later, Paul merged onto South U.S. 23 with both lanes packed, and by 4:45 he was on the Plymouth Road exit to Ann Arbor. He arrived on the leafy main campus of the University of Michigan within minutes and found the dorm complex that provided the usual inexpensive accommodations for academic meeting attendants. The campus was quiet this time of year, a far cry from the hustle and bustle that would reappear in the fall.

He parked and found his room, where he showered and crashed for a half hour. Dressed in a RULI tee-shirt, jeans and boat shoes, he walked in the humid shade of the ancient maples to the conference center building in time for the start of the social mixer.

*Already crowded as hell,* he noted, with noisy blue-jean-and-sandal clad grad students from all over the country and overseas wasting no time looking for new contacts among their peers or cruising the big name scientists hoping to get their faces and names known for future postdoc opportunities. Paul grabbed a beer and started looking over people's heads for Dr. Perry, who didn't seem to be there yet. Neither were Withers and Bates, to Paul's relief.

After chatting briefly with a couple of students he knew, he stepped out into the main hallway to escape the roistering clamor gushing from the mixer room. *Good folks in there, but taking all that in is like trying to drink water from a fire hydrant.*

Waiting for Dr. Perry, Paul wondered again what his mentor would do when he learned about the plagiarism. Walter Perry was an excellent doctoral advisor in every way, but as he was pushing 70 and within sight of emeritus status, he might not be up to a messy battle in academic ethics at this point. *Well I'll soon find out,* thought Paul, as he saw six-foot-three Perry shambling toward him with an old friend from Woods Hole. Perry's long freckled face broke into a grin.

"Paul, just the man I'm looking for! Say hello to Edmond Fielding. Ed, this is my student Paul Tyson." Paul beamed and shook hands, momentarily speechless. *Good god, this guy's only the most famous phytoplankton man in marine science.* Both Perry and Fielding had made their marks primarily in the 1970s, 80s and 90s, but their superstar status at these meetings had continued on through the first decade of the new century.

"I'm honored, Dr. Fielding," Paul finally managed,

"Call me Ed, please, and it's a pleasure to meet you too. I've been following your excellent Lake Michigan work."

"Thanks. By the way, Dr. Perry, I need to talk to you about the data when you have a chance."

"Sure Paul, how about right now? Ed has some friends he wants to see at the mixer."

"Ayup – I'll just tack in here and do that," said Fielding in his Down East accent. "See you boys."

Tyson and Perry sat down on a couple of big leather lounge chairs in a corner of the lobby. Paul took a deep breath and pulled the journal issue out of his back pack. "Take a look at this new article by Withers and Bates."

"Yes, I was reading my copy on the plane up from Washington. It's pretty good, isn't it?"

"Yeah…a little too good. Don't the plankton data look familiar?'

"Well, not exactly – what do you mean?"

"I guess I'm a little behind on bringing you up to date on my recent experiments. Dr. Perry, those are my plankton data in their paper."

Perry's ruddy complexion faded to the color of oatmeal. "You can't be serious. Are you certain? Couldn't they have done similar experiments?"

"Not a chance. Like I told Joan on Thursday, I know my data. I'm the only one at the Institute who uses that graphics package. Over the dates involved, Ron was totally engrossed in his zooplankton experiments, and Dr. Bates' lab doesn't even have the equipment to do phytoplankton work." Paul slapped the journal shut and jammed it into the back pack. "No fucking way is that their work, pardon my French. Ron must have pulled my files from our lab computer."

A little of Perry's color returned, but you still could have pushed him over with a feather. "You're going to have to be very careful with this. You'll need to get together everything possible to support your contention. Meanwhile, avoid any confrontations until I can confer with Director Tollefson about how she will want us to proceed. I can't begin to tell you what a dangerous road this will be. Often nobody wins. I know of a case like this in which, when the dust settled from the brouhaha of university politics, the *victim's* career was ruined, not the plagiarizer's. As they say, it's awful hard to get the shit back in the horse. For the time being, like old Will Rogers once said, 'Never pass up a good chance to shut up.'"

Nodding slowly, Paul stared across the lobby and chewed his lower lip

Dr. Perry's knees creaked as he rose from his chair and said, "Well, I'll go and find Ed in the mixer."

Paul sat for a few minutes and then got up to return to the mixer himself. He took a couple of steps into the hallway but stopped when he saw Ron Withers and Dr. Bates coming in the front entrance at the other end. Withers was tall and slender, with light brown hair; Bates was short, prematurely gray and balding. Paul quickly turned and went out a side entrance. He walked down North University Avenue to a diner and got some dinner, and then returned to his dorm room for the night.

Monday morning at eight thirty, Paul was in the back row of a seminar room listening to Ron Withers deliver a presentation of the latest research in the Bates group. It was painful for Paul to be there, but he had to know if any more of his data were being used by Withers. Not so far, thankfully. Paul slipped out of the room during the question period and went to another room to get a good seat at the next talk there. Paul got a front row seat, but that did not help him concentrate on the talk. His mind was on Withers most of the time.

Shortly after 10:00 AM, Paul was delivering his own paper, *Effects of Global Warming on Phytoplankton Communities of Northern Lake Michigan*, in one of the larger seminar rooms. Still distracted from having seen Ron Withers earlier, Paul struggled to the conclusion of his talk. "So the combined effects of warming water from increasing atmospheric heat conduction, and declining pH caused by carbonic acid derived from increased dissolved $CO_2$ loading, are clearly driving the plankton toward lower phytoplankton diversity dominated by previously rare species, which likely is causing the zooplankton community to change significantly. Although Dr. Perry and I do not study the higher trophic levels of these communities, we would expect changes there as well, all the way into the fish populations. Thank you."

After the usual polite applause at these talks, the moderator rose and said, "We have a few minutes for questions."

A man in a jacket and tie stood up from an aisle seat, glanced from side to side as though all the jeans and sandals around him were the uniforms of a hostile guerrilla army, and launched into a question that instantly marked him as one of the right-wing media reporters who always seem to be around snapping at your heels at every public presentation involving evolution, stem cell research, or global warming. "How can you be so sure that your results are from so-called global warming? Now that 'Climategate' has discredited global warming science as a hoax..."

"Excuse me sir," Paul interrupted. "The only thing discredited in 'Climategate' was a few injudicious email messages involving opinions among a few individuals, who have since been exonerated of any scientific malfeasance, and the rest of the hundreds of scientists in the field had nothing whatsoever to do with it. The only hoax is the one being spun by the deniers.

"Now, in my talk you obviously missed or ignored the careful controls in our experiments. The data clearly indicate that the plankton community is responding specifically to the combination of higher temperature and lower pH, and nothing other than the increasing atmospheric carbon dioxide load is likely to be causing the simultaneous warming and acidification of the lake water. Are there other questions?"

The red-faced reporter sat down and tried to ignore the cold stares from the people around him.

An earnest and astute young student stood from the last row and said, "Quite a bit of the data you have shown us looks very much like some of the data in the paper by Withers and Bates in the current issue of JFOS. Can you explain that apparent duplication?"

Paul flushed. *Shit. Here we go.* He glanced down at Dr. Perry, who was sitting in the front row with his face fading back to the color of oatmeal. Paul clenched his teeth and glared at the young woman. But he managed to speak quietly. "Well, you will have to ask them that question. Our data were generated in experiments conducted by me with assistance from two of Dr. Perry's lab technicians."

The moderator quickly stood and said, "We need to move on to the final talk before the lunch break. Let's thank this speaker once again."

Taking his seat beside Dr. Perry, Paul heard not a word of the next presentation as his pulse pounded in his ears. At the lunch break they both got up and silently walked out of the room and down the hallway.

Turning into the cafeteria, Paul abruptly bumped into the back of none other than Ron Withers, who was standing at the end of the line with a tray and silverware in his hands. Paul's powder keg blew. The tray and silverware crashed to the floor as he yanked Withers around by the arm and slammed him hard against the wall with a fistful of shirt at Ron's throat.

"YOU SON OF A BITCH, COME CLEAN ABOUT STEALING MY DATA, AND RETRACT YOUR ARTICLE, OR SO HELP ME I'LL BREAK YOUR FUCKING NECK."

In the sudden silence of a hundred staring eyes, Dr. Perry grabbed Paul from behind and gently pulled him away from Withers. A cafeteria full of people had heard every word.

# CHAPTER 4

Paul realized immediately that staying at the meeting for the rest of the week had become untenable. As Dr. Perry had planned to ride back to Traverse City with Paul, Perry reluctantly agreed to leave right away. They walked to the dorm, packed their bags, and went together to Paul's car for the drive north to Traverse City. They were mostly silent, but during a hasty lunch stop in Flint, Dr. Perry broached the obvious subject.

"Well, the cat is most certainly out of the bag now. And it's not exactly a house cat. I've got no experience as a lion tamer, Paul. Can you get yourself under control so we can pursue this properly?"

"You have my word, for what that's worth right now," said Paul as he finished a sodden French fry. He slid out of the booth and headed for the men's room.

Back on I-75, conversation continued to be sparse and strained as the miles crawled by. North of the Saginaw Bay Bridge, construction delays trapped them in dusty lines of cars and trucks with heat shimmering off their roofs and hoods. But Paul's attention was inward, where the heat of his anger at Ron Withers smoldered like a peat fire.

Finally reaching Traverse City after the hours on the road had seemed like days, Paul dropped Dr. Perry off at his car in the airport lot, and then drove on up to his boat in Elk Rapids. During that chilly evening aboard *Tondeleyo*, Paul decided to lay low for the rest of the week and try to think things through.

Paul did his best thinking while doing mindless chores on his boat, and so he got busy doing some sanding and painting on the cabin trunk. One day he dropped his dinghy into the water and worked his way around the boat touching up the gold stripe just below the rail. The fancy scrolls at the bow and stern ends of the stripe demanded his particular attention, which he welcomed wholeheartedly. He got the entire striping back to its stunning contrast to the gleaming black of the hull and the bright white of the cabin top and cockpit bimini.

Another day he cleaned the AC generator, changed its oil, and replaced a couple of worn wires. On yet another day, he lubricated the roller furling jib hardware and the winches. There were no fewer than seven winches on *Tondeleyo.*

Each day, after a couple of hour's work in the morning, he would knock off and stroll a block up to River Street for lunch at his favorite pizza-and-sandwich shop. One slice of pizza and half an Italian sandwich. Good as you could get anywhere. Taking his time, he would gaze out into the sun-washed street, and most days he would see a parade of tourists shuffle by. One day he paid particular attention to a family slurping away on triple scoop ice cream cones. Probably the ice cream had been preceded by a whole pizza each and a couple of whole sandwiches each. *And a diet soda, right? Big help. I should invest in diabetes drug companies, even though their stuff offers little help to anyone with that lifestyle. They just don't get it.* Paul was startled to find himself getting angry about the state of health of Americans. *Christ. Get a grip.*

In the afternoons he was back on the boat for several more hours of work in the perfect Michigan June weather. Cool breezes off the bay raised a soft chorus of halyards clinking against aluminum masts. Pale sunlight danced on the ripples decorating the harbor water, and impossibly white gulls glided above the sandbars in search of crayfish. About four p.m. each day Paul would grab an apple and climb the grassy hill to the library to read the papers and magazines for an hour on the porch overlooking the bay. On cue, the sun would begin to slant in from the west, highlighting the mastheads in the harbor. The scene should have been an elixir for the darkest of moods, but it was no match for Paul's brooding as day after day he could not come up with a viable plan to prove that Withers had stolen his data.

On Friday Paul finally decided to call Joan, and flipped open his cell phone.

"How were the meetings?" she asked.

"Fine, until about noon on Monday, when the shit sort of hit the fan."

After Paul described what had happened, Joan did not speak for a full minute.

"You've been back all week and haven't called till now?"

"I knew how busy you are with those tricky gene probes, and I didn't want to ruin your concentration with all this…especially when I have no answers for all the obvious questions. I just needed to work and think. But it hasn't helped. If you can forgive me for hiding out like this, I wouldn't mind some company right about now."

"I'll be there in an hour. Get the beer cold."

"It is."

Paul got out some steaks to thaw and was setting up the grill on the stern railing when Dr. Perry pulled into the harbor parking lot. He waved as he worked his lanky frame down the embankment and out along Paul's finger dock. Paul gave him a hand into the cockpit.

"Welcome aboard. Buy you a beer?"

"Thanks, but not now. Paul, I've met with Director Tollefson. She wants us to submit a written academic misconduct charge for her to file with the provost to initiate an official investigation. She was not happy to hear about the Ann Arbor incident, and insists on absolutely no more public comment during the due process. I told her we would hold to that. We will, won't we Paul?"

"Yes, we will. But I worry about pressing this official charge. I don't know how to make it stick. My original data books are missing. You and I know who has them, or destroyed them, but how do we prove that?"

"Look Paul, you are a fine young scientist, and a damn good man altogether for that matter. Don't tarnish that by reacting the wrong way in this thing. We'll figure this out. For one thing, as you said in Ann Arbor, my two lab techs helped you with your work. Their testimony will help."

"Well, thanks Dr. Perry. I will keep my trap shut. The last thing I want is to embarrass you again."

"Don't worry about me. Just take it easy on this next cruise. I'll start on a draft of the damned misconduct filing, and we can finish it when you get back." With that, Dr. Perry returned to his car, pulled out of the lot and headed back toward home in Traverse City.

That evening, after grilled steaks and a couple of cold ones, Paul and Joan tried to enjoy an early showing of the movie up on River Street. But even Steve Martin at his best could not bring a smile to Paul's face. After the film they walked along River Street and browsed the small shops and galleries. There were countless shelves and racks of hats, tee shirts and sweatshirts emblazoned with Elk Lake and Elk Rapids logos, and all sorts of nautical and north woods bric-a-brac. Artwork ranged from rather poor to rather good, some with surprisingly high prices for such unknown artists. Paul moped past all of it.

As they walked arm in arm back down to the harbor, Joan asked, "Where is that cheerful guy I knew last week?"

"Right now I'm thinking about the *Halcyon* cruise starting tomorrow, a whole week aboard with both Withers and Dr. Bates. And under orders to keep my big mouth shut the whole time."

It was now fully dark, and Paul flipped on the deck lights as they climbed aboard *Tondeleyo*.

"Can't you skip the trip?"

"How? My summer stipend from the institute is for service as a research technician on *Halcyon*. I can't refuse a cruise because I'm pissed at somebody. Maybe after Dr. Perry and I file our official charges, the institute will modify my cruise schedule to avoid Withers and Bates, but that hasn't happened yet. So I will be shipmates with a guy I'd like to throw off the fantail."

"Oh sure, Paul. Look, you'll just have to trust Dr. Perry to help get this straightened out. You'll be okay. Now, I should go home so you can pack and get ready to make their usual early morning cast off."

"I guess you're right. Thanks for coming, and sorry I'm such lousy company right now."

Joan gave Paul a lingering kiss, and then climbed over the lifelines to the finger dock and walked up to her Blazer. A quick wave, and she was gone. Paul shut off the deck lights and went below to pack.

# Chapter 5

It was a clear Saturday morning on June 12. Sunlight rose over the vineyards of Mission Point and washed into the West Arm of the bay. A west wind blew at 15 knots across the institute docks, and flags on *Halcyon's* jack staff snapped with the sound of popping corn.

"A bit breezy, but it's not supposed to blow much harder," said Dr. Bates, the chief scientist for this cruise.

Next to him on the bridge, First Mate Irv Thompson nodded, but frowned as he replied, "So they say. Is everyone aboard?"

"There's one more…oh there he is now."

As Paul Tyson approached along the dock with his sea bag, Dr. Bates brusquely turned aft and ducked through the door to his chief scientist cabin, the port-side twin of the captain's cabin to starboard. Both staterooms had portholes looking out both abeam and aft along the lifeboat deck. At the small desk bolted to the aft bulkhead, Bates sat down to his computer and booted it up.

Most of the rest of the scientific staff were lounging around the large foredeck with mugs of coffee as Paul stepped aboard, the wind flapping his carpenter jeans and plastering his raised jacket collar to the back of his neck.

"Well aren't we punctual now," cracked Ron Withers from the starboard bow rail. Paul paused. His jaw clamped and his face flushed, but he kept his eyes straight ahead and said nothing. He crossed the deck to the open forecastle hatch and disappeared below. Everyone on deck heard Paul slam his sea bag onto an empty bunk, and everyone saw the lingering smirk on Ron Withers' face before they got busy studying the wooden deck planks at their feet. Those who were not at the Ann Arbor meeting had heard all about last Monday's scuffle from those who were there.

Paul heard the scraping of the gangway being hauled onto the deck above him as he hurried aft below decks. He climbed the stairs to the galley for a coffee and brought the steaming mug forward up the next set of stairs to the bridge. Nodding to Captain Robado, who had just emerged from his cabin, Paul went out the portside door and walked aft along the lifelines of the deserted lifeboat deck.

He sat down on the deck and leaned against the hull of the lifeboat, facing out through the lifelines to port. The orange lifeboat was twenty-five feet long, and was strapped down on chocks and covered with canvas. There were a couple of feet of deck space between the lifeboat and the lifelines. This was Paul's favorite place to pass free time during *Halcyon's* sea passages, sometimes reading, sometimes daydreaming, sometimes napping on the deck. There would be little to do this morning until *Halcyon* reached the first sampling station of the day's run.

Mate Thompson leaned out of the bridge window and called for the deck crew to cast off. Seagulls exploded off the pilings and clawed for altitude as *Halcyon's* big hawsers rumbled aboard. Ringing for slow reverse, Thompson ordered hard left rudder to back her around into position to proceed forward out of the harbor. A prolonged horn blast sounded for "leaving berth", and *Halcyon* was on her way.

Sheltered by the Leelanau Peninsula, the west side of Traverse Bay was only slightly choppy, and the ride would be gentle for the entire thirty-mile run northward up the bay. But the wind was chilly, and most of the students on the foredeck retreated into the wardroom to ride out the run to the first station. They sat around the long settee drinking coffee, trading old jokes and complaining about the calculus requirement in the curriculum. Periodically the cook, Frank "Tiny" Palatine, came by and collected empty coffee mugs.

Tiny's nickname was derived partly from the sound of the last syllable of his surname, but mostly as a paradox to his immense size, especially around the middle. He habitually patted himself on the belly as he walked among the students. Today, one of the female students made the mistake of commenting to him that he seemed proud of that big belly. Tiny was apparently waiting for just such a comment. He stopped beside her and grinned.

"That's my elephant. Want to see its trunk?"

The young woman did not miss a beat.

"Not particularly. It's how you got the name 'Tiny', right?"

The old navy cook retreated to the galley in a barrage of laughter from the students, muttering something about these smartass new-age women. Not realizing he had gotten off easy, Tiny had no clue that the student probably could get him fired for sexual harassment if she wanted to.

Nearly three hours into the northward run, Paul was watching a cloudbank gathering from the west. The pilothouse door banged shut and Paul jerked his head to his right, where he saw Ron Withers coming aft from the doorway. Withers saw Paul at the same moment, and Withers dropped his eyes to the deck immediately. To avoid Paul, Withers proceeded aft on the inboard side of the lifeboat.

Paul stood up and moved aft along the lifelines to where he could see around the stern of the lifeboat, and watched Withers approach the ladder at the aft end of the boat deck. Paul now noticed a small navy-blue backpack over Withers' shoulder. Unusual to be carrying a backpack around the ship in the middle of a sea passage, especially for Withers, who didn't usually carry one anytime, as far as Paul remembered. *Whatcha got in there dude?* Seething now, Paul gripped the lifeboat davit with both hands, holding himself back. The urge to follow Withers down that ladder was blurring Paul's memory of promising Dr. Perry he would stay in control. Paul gripped the davit, ignoring the growing pain in his cramped hands.

In the pilothouse, Dr. Bates continued working on his grant proposal at his desk, and the captain and mate kept watch on the darkening cloud bank to the west. The mate switched to the WX weather channel on the VHF to get an update on the forecast.

Fifteen minutes later, *Halcyon* passed beyond the lee of Lighthouse Point into the full brunt of the wind, where four- to five-foot waves swept in from the west. Before turning left into the wind on her cross-lake course, *Halcyon* had to clear the shoals off Grand Traverse Light, and she was in the trough rolling heavily for at least ten minutes, far longer than Tiny the cook was willing to tolerate. Hatches and doors all over the ship were banging as two dozen eggs were launched off the galley counter and scrambled themselves on the galley deck around Tiny's feet, the yellow goop flowing back and forth all the way from port to starboard.

"JESUS CHRIST. GET THIS THING OUT OF THE GODDAMN TROUGH. WHO THE HELL'S DRIVING UP THERE?"

Tiny's tirade echoed all the way up to the bridge, and Cap grinned at the mate. "Tiny knew the float plan; can I help it if he never seems to get secure down there soon enough?"

In defense of the old navy cook's predictable outburst, he was used to big ships. "Not this silly little tub that rocks on her round old bottom like a ten dollar whore," he often said.

After turning and settling on her westerly course, *Halcyon* rode pretty well, with only moderate fore and aft pitching, and that was the expected condition for the long run across Lake Michigan. But the forecast was wrong, and a front that was supposed to pass to the south began shifting to a more northerly route. Two hours west of Leelanau, the pounding *Halcyon* was firmly in the grip of an intensifying wind storm.

In conditions like this, Captain Robado became irritated at the lack of respect for the Great Lakes that so many people had, especially open-ocean merchant mariners unfamiliar with the sea states that could develop here. Fact was, the many hundreds of ships, including ocean freighters, on the bottom of all of the big lakes were silent testimony to the ferocity that could equal almost anything the "salties" might encounter.

The *Halcyon* was not in danger at the moment, but the storm raged on with increasing fury.

# CHAPTER 6

Twenty minutes later the *Halcyon* shuddered as a ten foot wave slammed into her bow like a cannon shot, and blue water streamed over her foredeck. The mate flinched as bullets of windblown spray splattered the pilot house windows.

"Wasn't supposed to blow this hard today," shouted the helmsman over the shriek of the wind in the rigging.

"Only fools and newcomers predict the weather on the Great Lakes," mate Irv Thompson hollered back.

The helmsman continued to muscle the big forty-inch wheel, while Thompson held on to the overhead handrail and wondered when the scientific staff would get around to deciding to scratch this cruise. With 25-knot winds gusting to 35, working over the side while drifting sideways in the trough would be out of the question. The ship did not have modern bow- and stern-thrusters to keep her head-to-wind, and even then it would be too rough to work. Just then the captain burst onto the bridge from the stairway and struggled across the heaving deck to the mate, who was startled by the captain's red face and blazing eyes. "What's up Cap? This weather's not all *that* bad is it?"

Through clenched teeth, Captain Robado uttered the unthinkable: "We have to reverse course and do a man overboard search, IMMEDIATELY." He went to the telegraph pedestal and rang back from Ahead Full to Ahead Slow, and then said "Irv, I want you to take the wheel yourself and do a Williamson Turn to get us exactly onto the reciprocal of our track. After you get her around through that bitch of a trough and on course, put John back on the wheel. Then get your eyes on that water."

"Will do, Cap, but who went over?" Thompson asked.

"I'm told that Ron Withers is missing. No one saw anything, but they can't find him anywhere, and we have to assume he's in the water back there somewhere. And there's another thing. Word is that Withers and Paul Tyson have been having some kind of a tiff, and until we get all this under control, we need to get Tyson under observation." As the ship gradually lost speed, Captain Robado reached overhead for the VHF microphone and switched the radio to channel 16.

"MAYDAY, MAYDAY, MAYDAY. This is Research Vessel *Halcyon*. I have a possible man overboard situation. I am seven miles due north of North Manitou Island." Cap was looking at the chart plotter. "GPS coordinates are forty-five degrees, fourteen point four six two minutes North; eighty-five degrees, fifty point nine nine one minutes West. Over."

Within seconds a reply crackled out of the VHF speaker.

"*Halcyon*, Coast Guard Air Station Traverse City. How many are overboard, and what is your present action? Over."

"Air Station TC, we have one man missing. Unfortunately we are not sure where he may have gone over. We came up West Bay from Traverse City and have been on course 270 since rounding Grand Traverse Light. We are reversing course to 090 to retrace our outbound track to look for him. Over."

"Copy that, *Halcyon*. We will deploy two helicopter search and rescue units, one directly to your location to backtrack with you, and the other one starting northbound out of Traverse City. Also will request the sheriff's marine division to deploy surface rescue craft, but in the present sea state they will have to stay in the bay. Over."

"Thanks TC. One more thing. We need a marine security officer standing by at the Institute dock to interrogate a 'person of interest,' over."

"Will do, Captain. Choppers and surface vessels will all be standing by on 16. Air Station Traverse City out."

"*Halcyon* out and standing by."

Mate Thompson had heard all of it. "Christ, Cap, they're just grad students. Come to think of it, I did notice Tyson was a little grumpy this morning. But I can't believe…"

"It's about stolen research data or something, but Irv, just get going on the turn. Withers could be anywhere back there. I'm going below to arrange lookout watches."

Captain Robado found the second mate in the wardroom, explained the situation and told him to get the chief engineer and find Paul Tyson.

"Bring Tyson to the wardroom and have the chief stay with him."

"Will do, Cap."

Robado went out on deck, where the students and deckhands already had their eyes glued on the water. He sent two deckhands up to the pilothouse and instructed them to get binoculars from the mate and scan the water out to the horizon on each side of the ship. He put three students at the bow and told them to concentrate forward on the ship's heading. He put two students up on the boat deck, one on each side, to watch alongside and in the middle distance. The remaining student was to search every possible space within the ship in the dwindling hope that Withers was still aboard somewhere.

After the mate got the *Halcyon* turned around back eastward, she was riding much easier downwind, although she was still pitching and yawing some from the following seas. The mate and the chief were making their way along the boat deck aft of the pilot house when they found Paul Tyson. Paul was sitting against the lifeboat, staring seaward past the lifelines and rubbing the side of his head.

"What's wrong with your head, Tyson?" asked the mate.

"Banged it on the fucking stanchion when we rolled in the trough back there. What the hell did we turn around for?"

"Ron Withers is missing. Cap wants to know if you know anything about that. Wants you in the wardroom ASAP. So you need to come with us."

Paul's eyes widened and rolled skyward. He drew a deep breath, grabbed the top lifeline, and slowly pulled himself up. "Lead on."

Steadying themselves on the lifelines, the three of them walked forward to the pilot house. They entered the bridge and walked past the silent stares of the crew, who returned quickly to their lookout duties. They continued down through the galley into the wardroom, where the second mate asked the chief to stand by there with Tyson, and left to find the captain. Under the watchful eye of the chief, Paul Tyson sat back against the midship bulkhead in the wardroom and gazed across through a starboard porthole at the waves that were now following along with the ship at nearly the same speed.

The ship yawed forlornly along her downwind course back toward the Leelanau Peninsula and Grand Traverse Bay as Mate Thompson navigated *Halcyon* along the reciprocal course of her outbound track and communicated by radio with the helicopter crews. One of the helicopters roared overhead in a weaving search pattern along *Halcyon's* track.

"*RV Halcyon,* this is Coast Guard SAR unit 600Y," crackled *Halcyon's* VHF speaker. It was one of the 44 foot HH-65C "Dolphin" search and rescue helicopters.

"Go ahead 600Y," replied the mate.

"Any idea what the missing man is wearing?"

"We think it is a gray sweatshirt," said the mate.

"About the worst color for visibility in this water. We'll keep looking up here. CGNR 600Y out"

"Thanks. *Halcyon* out."

Mate Thompson could see the other chopper slowly searching over the bay to the east. The search wore on for two hours on the eastward run, with no results. Gloom settled over the ship, as all eyes silently roamed over the churning water until they glazed over with fatigue.

# Chapter 7

After passing Lighthouse Point, the mate turned *Halcyon* south, rolling violently in the trough again until reaching the lee of the peninsula. She made her way quietly down the calmer bay, still searching for Ron Withers. The two Coast Guard helicopters had zig-zagged along *Halcyon's* original track countless times, and one of them was now searching eastward downwind of the Grand Traverse Light all the way across the head of the bay, but there was no sign of Withers anywhere. By now the cold front had brought dark clouds in over the bay to match the mood aboard *Halcyon*.

Paul Tyson was dozing in his seat when the quiet of the wardroom was shattered by a shriek from somewhere below deck.

"OH MY GOD. OH MY GOD. I FOUND HIM. CAPTAIN! SOMEBODY HELP. HE'S NOT MOVING. OH MY GOD," cried one of the research techs as she rushed up the stairway into the galley.

The captain and the chief engineer had just entered the galley from forward, and they followed the frantic student back down the stairs and aft through the chemistry lab into a small storage room. She pointed her shaking hand to the deck hatch at her feet.

The mate lifted the hatch and swung it up and over to its fully open position. They stared down and saw Ron Withers sprawled face down in the shallow hold. He was utterly still, and the dim light accentuated his fish belly pallor. Captain Robado stepped down into the hold beside Withers and felt his neck for a pulse. At first there seemed to be none, but then Cap did feel one – feint and rapid as though in a small bird. Cap leaned very close and just barely felt Ron's moist breath, slow and shallow. He pressed gently on Ron's shoulder. "Ron. Ron. Can you hear me?"

Silence.

"Give me your flashlight, Chief." The stark white beam roved over the young man's body, and came to rest on the dark red stain spreading in the light brown hair on the back of Withers' head. Cap carefully felt the skull around that area, aware that he should have a glove on to avoid contact with the blood, but what the hell. Cap stood up.

"He's alive, but barely. Awful blow to his head. No other injuries, I think. Chief, stay here and keep checking for pulse and breathing. If either one stops, turn him over and start CPR. But be careful chief, the back of his skull is all loose and mushy. I'm going up to get on the radio, and I'll send someone down with the cardio zapper in case you lose him."

"Will do, Cap. Jesus fucking Christ."

On his way forward Captain Robado bumped into Dr. Bates, who was hesitantly approaching the storage room, and told him to find a deck hand and send him back with the defibrillator unit.

On his way to the bridge, Robado gave a silent shake of his head as he stepped past the group of stunned students and techs in the galley. On the bridge, he simply shook his head at Mate Thompson, and then keyed the VHF mike.

"Traverse City search units, this is *Halcyon*. We have found the missing man aboard ship. Repeat to all units, we have found the missing man aboard *Halcyon*. Ronald Withers is gravely injured with head trauma. We are monitoring as best we can, but we need professional assistance and a medical evacuation immediately. Over."

"*Halcyon,* CGNR 600Y. We copy. We are just a mile behind you. We need you to steer a course that will keep the wind at thirty degrees to starboard of your bow, and maintain a speed of seven knots. We will hold position above you and lower a basket and a rescue swimmer team to your foredeck. They are qualified for paramedic duty. Notify us when you are ready. Over"

"Roger that, 600Y."

Cap told the mate to ring the engine room for Ahead Half and to turn fifteen degrees to starboard. Then he called the Coast Guard Air Station headquarters.

"Air Station TC, I assume you heard my conversation with the chopper. I reaffirm my earlier request that appropriate investigation officers be present when we arrive at the institute dock. I expect to be there in about one hour, depending on the duration of the chopper transfer."

"We copy, *Halcyon.* The hospital is standing by. Air Station Traverse City out."

Captain Robado then hailed the institute marine operations superintendent, David Washington, who was monitoring channel 16. "Dave, I assume you have heard all of this. I also assume you know who the person of interest is, and why."

"Yeah, Cap, we know, and let's just leave it at that here on the open radio. We're ready and waiting. As I'm sure you are aware, you need to alert everyone there that every person aboard will need to give a statement to the authorities, probably more than once, but certainly before they leave the ship. See you shortly. RULI headquarters out."

Cap keyed the mike once again. "CGNR 600Y, *Halcyon* is maintaining requested course and speed. Over."

"Copy, *Halcyon,*" crackled the VHF.

Cap sent the mate down to supervise the transfer, and remained on the bridge to keep *Halcyon* on station. The clattering chopper hovered into position, and the two Coast Guard swimmers with a rescue basket slowly descended on a cable toward the foredeck. The gale-force rotor wash battered the mate and his deck hand, their ball caps blown like November leaves out over the water into the gray gloom. Fifteen minutes later the chopper hoisted its crew and Ron Withers, heavily bound in the basket, up into its cargo bay. The fat orange bird swiveled around, canted its head down and pounded off southward. Captain Robado watched it through the rattling windows while getting *Halcyon* back on her southerly course and back up to cruising speed. When Mate Thompson arrived back on the bridge, Cap asked him to go down and inform all hands, both scientific and ship's crew, that they will be asked for statements by the authorities on arrival. "Also, ask Chief Jordan to keep an eye on Paul Tyson in the wardroom, and then bring Dr. Bates up here with you."

"Yes, sir. Cap, I have to tell you that the swimmer medics won't be surprised if Withers winds up DOA at the hospital."

"Yep. Well, get below Irv. There's lots to do."

When the mate returned with Dr. Bates, Robado turned the bridge watch over to Thompson. Cap entered his cabin with Dr. Bates in tow, and closed the door. "Have a seat Dr. Bates. We obviously have a disaster here. First of all, the search. That storage room and the hold are in the scientific area. Why didn't someone look there sooner? Time is critical for Withers."

"Cap, that hold is small and only has older equipment in need of repair, none of which would have been needed on this cruise. I checked that myself yesterday while prepping for the trip. There would have been no reason for Ron or anyone else to be down in there. In fact I thought it was locked. It's surprising, but lucky, that Rachel looked in there when she did."

"Lucky yes," Robado nodded, "But that is a pretty feeble reason not to look there immediately, under these conditions. Now, even though that hold is in the scientific area and generally the chief scientist's responsibility, every square foot of a ship is ultimately the captain's responsibility. I don't know where this will come down for you, but you must know that I could well lose my job before this is over."

"God, I hope not Cap. You couldn't have…"

"Bates," Cap interrupted, "can any of your people account for where Paul Tyson was during the time that Withers became missing?"

"Not to my knowledge."

"Can you?"

Dr. Bates abruptly stood to leave. "No, I can't."

In the wardroom, Paul Tyson had seen the loaded rescue basket as the crew struggled with it up through the galley and out on deck. He sat waiting while *Halcyon* steamed the rest of the way down the West Arm to Traverse City, with his elbows on the table, thumbs under his chin, and eyes in a thousand-yard stare. Leaning nearby against the galley door, Chief Jordan was tapping his knee brace against the door jamb. Finally he asked, "You need to hit the head before we get in? Whoa, bad choice of words there. Well anyway, do you need to go?"

Paul gave the chief a smoldering stare, and replied "You going to hold it for me and everything?"

"Sorry Tyson. Look, I was told to keep an eye on you. I guess Cap doesn't want you jumping overboard before we get in, eh?"

"Oh sure, with two police Zodiacs and a Coast Guard chopper tailing us like gulls after a garbage scow." *But you're not way off base, Chief. It did come to mind for a while there.* Paul rose to go relieve his aching bladder, his heart flopping around in his chest like a rock bass in a rowboat.

# CHAPTER 8

Joan Brockton was passing by the open door of the institute marine operations office when the crackling voice from the VHF radio receiver stopped her in her tracks. She was overhearing parts of David Washington's radio exchange with the *Halcyon*. "Ron Withers gravely injured...person of interest...arriving soon...criminal investigation officers...."

Joan walked outside, stumbled down the main dock and sat down on a bollard to wait for Paul. She didn't know if they would even let her talk to him, but she had to try. *I was afraid there might be some trouble, but nothing like this. Paul's about to be arrested as a damn criminal.* Joan had not prayed since she was a very young girl; she silently tried to now. *If there's anyone up there, please make it be that Paul did not do this. He is too good to have done this. Isn't he?*

"WELL ISN'T HE?" she cried out into the darkening windy harbor. There was no echo, and there was no answer.

Minutes later, sirens wailed from half a mile away as the official vehicles approached the institute. Joan's breath caught in her throat when she saw Director Tollefson, Superintendent Washington, and Dr. Perry coming out of the limnology building, and again when five black Crown Victoria Interceptors squealed into the parking lot and rolled to a stop on the dock. The five sets of blinding blue rotators had the whole waterfront pulsing like a dance floor in a Saturday night roadhouse. But the sirens fell silent, and the only tune Joan heard was the incessant wind in the halyards of the institute's flagstaffs that flew the state flag, the institute flag, and the small craft warning.

The blue flashes flickered back off of *Halcyon's* pilot house as she finally approached out of the dark haze. Two deckhands were visible on deck as the reverse prop wash boiled out from under *Halcyon's* counter to stop her along her berth.

"Excuse me miss," said the seaman preparing to drop the open loop of the stern hawser onto the bollard that Joan was sitting on.

"Oh yeah, sorry," she said. She jumped up and moved to the other side of the dock to watch the cluster of officials waiting for the gangway to be hauled into place. Then they boarded: the three institute principals, four police officers and a crime scene forensic team, and a county marine inspector with the two chopper medics who had evacuated Ron Withers.

The inspector from the marine division immediately took charge aboard *Halcyon*. After sending two of the deputies with Paul Tyson to wait up in the captain's cabin, he said "I want the captain, mate, chief engineer, and chief scientist in the wardroom, along with the medics and the forensic team. I want all other ship's personnel standing by on the foredeck with this officer until I clear the wardroom. Officer Burris, is it? See that no one leaves, and no one else comes aboard. Okay, all other officials please join us in the ward room. After a few minutes they all got sorted out, introduced to each other, and settled down. The inspector began.

"Before we start, let me report that at this time Mr. Withers is alive but critical and comatose in the ICU at the hospital. He has severe trauma to the back of his skull, a massive hematoma, and will undergo surgery soon. My cell phone will receive calls of any changes. Now before the forensic team gets started below, let us establish what is known here. First, what were the circumstances of Mr. Withers' injury when he was found?"

Captain Robado stated, and Chief Jordan and the two coast guard medics all agreed, that Withers was found face down and totally unconscious. His position indicated that he was not injured by falling into the hold, because the injury was in back. If he had fallen in backwards, the severity of the injury, meaning being knocked out cold immediately, probably would have prevented him from turning over on his face later. Either way, he would have been unlikely, and probably unable, to close the big hatch after falling in. Furthermore, the hold was only a three feet deep crawl space, and he was on top of some old life jackets that would have cushioned a fall from that height.

During this discussion, Dr. Bates pulled a digital camera out of his shirt pocket, and showed the inspector a photo he had taken of Withers in the hold. Bates had gone up to his cabin for the camera after sending the deckhand down with the cardio unit. The inspector took a long look, and then passed the camera around the ward room. When Dr. Perry saw it, his oatmeal pallor crept back.

"I gather," the inspector continued, "that no one here thinks Mr. Withers could have been injured by himself in that situation." No one spoke; several nodded in agreement. "So we seem to have blunt object trauma that may have been perpetrated by someone else." said the inspector. Again no one said anything, but several nodded. "In that case, I ask the forensic team to follow the chief engineer to the scene and begin a search for a weapon, obviously to include the entire ship. Of course we know that if there is such a weapon it could by now be floating somewhere on northern Lake Michigan, or lying on the bottom. But the search must be made." The team and the chief rose and started for the stairway.

"Now, why are we holding this Mr. Tyson as a person of interest?"

Dr. Bates cleared his throat and said, "Because Tyson threatened Ron in Ann Arbor last Monday. Threatened to break his neck in fact."

"Why did he do that?"

Now Dr. Perry jumped in, "Because he was convinced that Withers has plagiarized him in a publication. But surely he was speaking only figuratively!" Perry and Bates exchanged stony stares.

The inspector started to ask how something like that could evoke such violence, but Director Tollefson interrupted him.

"Inspector, with all respect, that matter is indeed very serious, but it is a confidential matter pending investigation in the university," she paused, raised questioning eyebrows at Dr. Perry, and got a nod from him, "and we cannot discuss it further at this time."

"Well, okay," said the inspector. "But it does appear that we have a viable motive. What about opportunity? I guess I address this to the chief scientist. When was Withers last seen by anyone?"

Dr. Bates said, "A couple of the techs saw him go down the forecastle hatch about fifteen minutes before we rounded Lighthouse Point, but no one saw him after that, as far as I know."

"Was Tyson seen anywhere near Withers around that time?"

"No one has reported that," answered Dr. Bates.

"Were Tyson's whereabouts known at all, by anyone, around the time that Withers became missing?"

"No one has reported that either," answered Dr. Bates, who was now studying the pattern in the table top beneath his hands.

The inspector looked around the wardroom. Silence. "So we cannot rule out the opportunity for Mr. Tyson to have been involved in this possible crime. Under the circumstances, I think we must ask the district judge to arraign him for suspicion of assault with intent to commit murder."

Dr. Perry shot up off his seat and said, "Wait a minute, that is utterly excessive! This is completely circumstantial. You've got no weapon and no witnesses."

"Dr. Perry, we have a victim near death, probable foul play, and a suspect with a motive. The prosecution always enters the strongest relevant charges, and the investigations and the case proceed from there. I have no choice."

Perry nodded slowly, grabbing the edge of the table as though he was losing his balance. "Well, can you please have Paul's sea bag cleared so I can take it with me?"

"Yes, we can do that. Now I want the university officials and ship's officers to leave the wardroom to make room for the rest of the ship's crew and scientific staff. Each of them is to write a statement of events as they saw them today. Can we get them paper and pens?"

Mate Thompson nodded.

"I will now interrogate Mr. Tyson," the inspector continued. "Captain, would you please escort me to your stateroom?"

Everyone rose, and Dr. Perry trudged below to find the forensic team. Paul's sea bag contained only some clothes and a small dopp kit, and Perry was allowed to take it up on deck to wait until everyone was released from the ship.

In the captain's stateroom, the inspector read Paul his Miranda rights, and then began the questions.

"Mr. Tyson, what happened today?"

Paul took a deep breath. "We were steaming along, getting beat up pretty bad out there, when all of a sudden all hell broke loose and I got hauled down here like I was dog that ate a baby."

"Where were you during the trip?"

"Up on the boat deck beside the lifeboat."

"Beside the lifeboat? Doing what exactly?"

"Sleeping, mostly."

"You were sleeping by the lifeboat. How could you sleep in that windstorm?

"I've had lots of practice."

"Anyone see you doing this?"

"How would I know?"

"Did you have any contact with Ron Withers? Did you slip down there and lay a pipe or a board to the back of his head like you said you would last Monday?"

"Your people will never find any pipe or board with my DNA on it, I'll tell you that. I don't hunt people down in my sleep."

"How about when you are awake?"

Paul leveled his gaze directly into the inspector's eyes, and did not blink until the inspector looked away.

"I think I need legal representation," Paul said.

"That you do," said the inspector. "Mr. Tyson, we are going to have to take you downtown and read you in for suspicion of assault with intent to commit murder. Withers may not make it through the night. Officer, please cuff Mr. Tyson, take him to your squad car and wait for us. And send in the rest of the people on the foredeck so I can try to crosscheck some of these facts."

The inspector went back down to the wardroom to interview the crew and the students.

# Chapter 9

Outside, the wind had finally calmed down somewhat, but it had begun to rain. Joan was standing now beside the ship. She had the hood of her windbreaker up, but it was not waterproof, and she was getting wet. All five racks of squad car lights were still flashing frantically, and now blue reflections were dancing off rainwater puddles all over the dock. Joan stared at them until she became disoriented and nearly swayed off the dock. She caught herself, shook her head, and blinked a few times. *Why don't the cops ever turn those damn things OFF. They're HERE for Christ sake.* Then she saw Paul shuffling across the gangway. At the sight of his wrists cuffed behind his back, all the air went out of her and everything inside seemed to come loose and slump down to her pelvic floor. She fought for breath as she stumbled over to him.

"Paul, what the hell...." She could say no more.

Paul stopped short, and the deputy bumped into his back. "They think I tried to put Ron's lights out. They're taking me downtown. I don't know when I will be able to see you. But Joan, keep an eye on Dr. Perry. He doesn't look so good."

"Let's go ... 'scuse us ma'm," said the officer.

Joan nodded, drew the back of her hand across her tear streaked cheeks, and turned to look for Dr. Perry.

The local TV station had heard the police scanner, and a remote transmitter van was now in the parking lot behind the squad cars. A camera man and a talking head got into position at the gangway, but no one would talk to them as people began to file quickly off of the ship. Dr. Perry was one of the first to leave. Joan took his arm, grabbed the sea bag, and walked with him toward the parking lot.

"This can't be happening," said Perry.

"I know, I know," Jane replied. "Are you alright? Look, why don't you ride with me to police headquarters. We're going to have to help get Paul out of there if we can. Don't they allow bail to be posted or something?"

"I guess it depends on how tight a case they think they have, and whether they can be sure he is not a 'flight risk,' as I think they call it."

"Well here's my truck," Joan said, and opened the door for Dr. Perry. By the time she got around into the driver's seat she had decided to take him to the hospital to get checked over before going to the station. She didn't like the way he was clutching at his left shoulder. She drove the Blazer out of the lot, blue cop lights still flashing back there.

At the police station, Paul went through the initial booking routine of mug shots, fingerprints and all the rest. "How about that traditional phone call I'm supposed to be able to make?" An officer pointed to the phone over on an empty desk by the wall. The handset was sticky and stank of cigarettes, booze and god knew what else from hundreds of other poor suckers who had made calls like this from here. Paul dialed the only lawyer he knew.

"Craig, this is Paul Tyson. I've got a problem."

"Paul, you old wharf rat! It's only nine o'clock on a Saturday night. I know you, and it's not late enough for you to have a problem yet. You're at a bar right? Remember that old Jerry Lee song? Just wait till closing time, and the girls will all get prettier." Craig Basham started singing.

"Craig...DUDE." The singing stopped. "Craig, if it were only that simple. Fact is, I'm in here at police headquarters getting booked for suspicion of attempted murder."

"Say WHAT?"

"You heard me right. Short of it is, I got pissed at a kid at the institute for publishing some of my data, and threatened him down in Ann Arbor last Monday. Today they found him on the *Halcyon* with his head caved in, and me on the same cruise with no alibi. Craig, I need legal help."

"What is a hal-see-on?"

"It's the name of the research ship, for Chrisake. Can you get over here?"

"Paul, I'm an environmental lawyer. I litigate *against* bad guys, the ones that dump shit in rivers and develop wetlands. Criminal law for me was one course in my second year of law school. You need a big name defense attorney."

"Can't afford a big name defense attorney."

"Can't afford me either, bro."

"Well, get yourself a pro bono merit badge by helping me out here, man."

Craig was silent for a few beats. "All right, Paul. I'll come over. But if and when it gets real rough, I will have to call in some backup."

"Fair enough, Craig."

"Okay. My office is just across the street, so I'll be there in a few minutes."

Paul hung up and said to the cops, "We're not going any farther with this until my big gun lawyer gets here."

But they had heard Paul's end of the conversation. "Some big gun," one of them cracked. "That was Craig Basham, right? We know who he is. Fuckin' tree hugger puke."

Paul stiffened. "Oh, so now I'm getting an appraisal of my legal staff from a tin horn goon cop with an IQ of his badge number."

The officer blinked and then looked down at his badge as though he had forgotten that it was number 23. He flushed and took a step toward Paul, but the other officers held him back. Officer 23 quickly regained his composure and stopped trying to advance on Paul. Then he said, "Put this college boy puke in the drunk tank. We got a couple good ol' boys in there that'll make him feel real welcome."

The officers led Paul through the door to the hallway and stopped in front of the first large cell. Two large young men in dirty sleeveless tee shirts were in there, one sitting on the floor against the back wall and the other sitting on a bench at a side wall. Both were holding their heads in their hands as though to prevent their beer-soaked brains from sloshing around too much. They stirred, and their bloodshot eyes perked up when Officer 23 spoke.

"Hey you rummies. We got a nice college boy here for you to play with. You be good company now, you hear?"

The two drunks looked at each other and grinned. They were unemployed common laborers who lived in an abandoned shack over in a jack pine stand between Traverse City and Fife Lake. They drove a battered old pickup, and had been bar hopping all day. But they hadn't been in a good fight yet today, and this was like throwing raw meat into a shark tank.

Officer 23 opened the cell door and shoved Paul inside. Paul looked at the two rednecks, and then looked back at Officer 23. "These your cousins, pea brain?" Officer 23 smirked as he locked the cell door, and all three officers went back out to the front and closed the hallway door.

"College boy, eh? Haven't busted one up in a while, have we Arty?" said Jake, the man on the bench.

"Nope," said the one on the floor, flexing his fingers.

Paul stared at them for a moment. Ignoring the look in Paul's eyes, the two drunks made four mistakes. Number one, they assumed that this "college boy" was some kind of wimp. Number two, they were still very drunk, while Paul was knife-edge sober and in full possession of his athletic skills. Number three, they assumed that they were the angriest, meanest dudes in the county, and had no inkling of Paul's mental state right now. Number four, they decided to take turns with Paul so as to double their pleasure. Very big mistakes. It was over very quickly.

Up off the floor now, Arty took the first turn and waded toward Paul, licking spittle from his lower lip. Paul easily sidelined him by feinting once with his left and then kicking him hard in the crotch. The man crumpled and rolled to the wall holding his ruined testicles and sucking air. He managed to wheeze out some words through clenched teeth.

"Get the fucker, Jake."

The man on the bench started to rise, but never made it upright. With a perfect tackle, Paul's shoulder drove him into the wall, ribs cracking like pistol shots and a lung collapsing like a wet popcorn bag. Paul grabbed the man's long oily hair and brought a knee into the man's face so hard that his nose shattered and he went down in a motionless heap.

Paul turned back to the other man, who was still against the wall with his arms between his legs. Just as Paul was aiming a kick to the man's kidneys, the hallway door burst open. Craig Basham strode through with the three officers close behind him. Officer 23 stared slack-jawed at the two rednecks incapacitated on the floor and Paul breathing hard but without a scratch on him.

"I want my client out of this drunk tank immediately," Craig seethed. Directly to Officer 23, he said, "I suppose you thought you were throwing a lamb to the lions."

Officer 23 unlocked the cell door and sneered at Paul. "Looks like we can add to the assault charges, right hot shot?"

"Oh yeah, like these big bad boys are going to want it known that one 'college boy' wimp took down the two of them," replied Paul.

Craig Basham ignored the comments and motioned for Paul to come out of the cell. While Officer 23 and a second officer tended to the men on the floor, the third officer led

Craig and Paul down the hall through another door toward an empty cell. Craig asked to be allowed to confer with his client in the cell. The officer checked Craig for weapons, locked Craig and Paul in the cell, and said he would be back in fifteen minutes. Craig and Paul sat down.

"Okay Paul, start at the beginning."

Craig Basham had been a pal of Paul's back in undergrad school at Northwestern. Craig had gone to law school when Paul started grad school, and they were later surprised and delighted to have both wound up in the Traverse City area. They got together now and then to knock back a few in the local brew pubs.

Basham had specialized in environmental law in school, and had done an internship at a small firm in southern Wisconsin. Finishing his law degree, he located an opening at a firm in Traverse City that had done environmental work in northern Michigan for many years. Craig advanced quickly, and had made partner in just seven years, never having lost a single case. And he had faced some of the wealthiest corporations and toughest judges in the state. He was already known as one of the best courtroom lawyers around. As for criminal law? Well, Paul had to hope that Craig Basham was still the fast learner he was when they were in college.

Craig listened very intently now to Paul's description of the past two weeks.

"It's really pretty simple. Two weeks ago I read a new journal article published by Ron Withers and Dr. Bates at the institute and found a bunch of my data in it. A whole bunch. Then I discovered that my data notebooks were missing. Down at the national meeting in Ann Arbor I lost it, made a big scene in the crowded cafeteria. Grabbed him and shouted something about breaking his fucking neck."

"Lovely," said Basham. "So you broadcasted a motive for yourself big-time."

"So it would seem. In fact, Dr. Perry and I are filing plagiarism charges with the university administration. An official motive, so to speak."

"Very lovely."

"Anyway, we were all on the *Halcyon* this morning heading out into the 'perfect storm.' Withers became missing, and then turned up in a heap below with massive head trauma. They came and got me on the boat deck and told me to pack up for jail."

Craig Basham thought for a moment.

"So where were you the whole time?"

"Sitting or napping on the boat deck beside the lifeboat."

"The whole time?"

"Yep."

"Napping?"

"Yep."

"In a storm?"

"Yep."

"Anyone see you there?"

"No idea."

Basham paused again.

"Am I supposed to believe you?"

"Look damn you…"

"Paul, ignore that last question. But this is not going to be easy. A hot temper will not make it any easier. Now, how can we find out if anyone saw you up there the whole time?"

Paul shrugged.

# Chapter 10

From the institute lot Joan had driven down U.S. 31 South past Front Street and turned right on Sixth Street toward the hospital. Dr. Perry said, "This isn't the way to the police station. Where are you going?"

"I want you to get checked over at the hospital first. You haven't been looking so good."

"What do you mean?"

"You're very pale, you're breathing hard, and you keep rubbing your left shoulder. To be blunt, I'm worried that you might be having a heart attack. This is a terrible stress for all of us, and, well…you're no spring chicken Dr. Perry."

"Oh my, do I look that bad?" said Perry. "I'm really okay Joan. This shoulder thing, I strained hell out of it yesterday moving some heavy rocks in my wife's garden. I might need to have it looked at, but it's no emergency. Let's not waste time with that now."

"It won't take long," said Joan as she pulled up to the emergency entrance of the hospital and shut off the engine. "Please forgive me, Dr. Perry, but I'm not leaving here until you get this checkup."

"Okay young lady. Let's go get it over with."

The emergency department was idle, and Dr. Perry was taken into an examination room immediately. After moving her Blazer to the parking lot, Joan sat in the lobby and alternately worried about Dr. Perry and about Paul. She tried to distract herself with a magazine, and had actually gotten part way through an article when Dr. Perry came out grinning. "Healthy as a horse, they said. ECG is normal. They gave me some Motrin for the shoulder and told me 'ice for forty-eight hours and then heat.' Let me give them my insurance info, and let's get on over to the police station."

Entering the police station lobby, Joan and Perry were told they could not see Mr. Tyson. Yes, they could wait to see his lawyer. No, they didn't know when he would be out. Ten minutes later, environmental attorney Craig Basham lumbered out of the hallway. Neither Joan nor Perry knew him, but they assumed he was Paul's lawyer.

A "tree hugger puke?" Well, Basham was six-one and two-thirty with a crew cut, and looked like he could wrap his arms around a big running back, drive him for a five yard loss and plow up some turf with his ass. Which is what he used to do on Saturday afternoons as a linebacker for Northwestern. Now, in his button-down shirt, khakis and loafers, he stopped in front of Joan and Dr. Perry, the only people there in the lobby.

"Hi, I'm Craig Basham. You must be Joan Brockton and Dr. Perry; Paul thought you would be here." Basham sat down. "Deal is this: they have booked Paul on suspicion of assault with intent to do great bodily harm. Ron Withers is undergoing surgery, and is still extremely critical. As Withers could die at any moment, in which case the charge would go to murder one, they are unwilling to release Paul until he is arraigned before a district judge on Monday. In the meantime Paul can see no one except me. You both had best go home, and I will call you first thing Monday when I learn what time he is to be arraigned."

"How is Paul?" asked Joan.

"Holding up okay, under the circumstances."

Dr. Perry asked, "Can they really arraign him with so little concrete evidence?"

"Yes, they feel that Paul's threat of violence to Withers in Ann Arbor and Paul's opportunity on the ship are enough to hold him for now. As for whether they can get an indictment on that basis, I have my doubts, but as you know, they are investigating now to try to fill in the holes in the case. On that subject, Paul tells me that the forensic team is going to have to plow through a very large number of things on that ship that could be viewed as a blunt object weapon. Is that right?"

"God yes," Perry said. "In addition to the usual ship's deck and engine room tools, many things in the scientific areas would be candidates: samplers, weights, coring pipes, tools, on and on. Galley stuff too, for that matter. If they have to examine all of those things for evidence of contact with Ron Withers' head, they are going to be at it for a long while, maybe weeks."

"Well, that will give us time to work on the defensive side," Basham replied.

Joan said, "But can he get out of jail in the meantime?"

"I'm pretty sure I can get him released on bond on Monday. That could change if Withers dies."

Dr. Perry winced and started rolling his left shoulder, but stopped when he saw Joan watching him.

"What should we do with Paul's sea bag?" said Perry.

"You can give it to me, and I'll keep it along with his personal effects that they gave me here in this envelope."

"Belt, watch, and stuff?" asked Joan. Basham nodded.

"Jesus Christ."

"Let's go to your car and get his bag," suggested Basham. "It's going to be okay."

Joan stared back. "By that do you mean that he didn't do it, or that you can get him off?"

"Both, I hope."

"He hopes?" muttered Joan to Dr. Perry as Basham went out the door. "Paul's future hinges on the hopes of this guy with a bent nose who looks more like a coach than a lawyer?"

Perry replied before they followed Basham outside.

"I hate to tell you this, but I think Paul told me he has a friend who is an environmental lawyer. This must be him."

"Oh great," said Joan.

They went out to join Craig Basham in the parking lot. It was still windy, but the rain had stopped.

Down the hall in his cell, Paul lay on the hard cot with his ankles crossed and hands behind his head, staring at the faded yellow ceiling. The room had begun to swirl slowly around him as the torrent of events carried him ever faster, totally beyond his control. Closing his eyes did not help.

That night Paul did not sleep, and all day Sunday he barely picked at his food. Craig Basham stopped by briefly in the afternoon to tell him that Ron Withers was hanging on at the hospital, and it looked like he just might make it.

*If he wakes up, will he have a memory?* wondered Paul.

On that Sunday, the wind storm had passed on eastward, but clouds and light rain remained. All day, Joan paced and fretted in her small efficiency apartment on Front Street, her mind spinning like a tin can on a rifle range. She was only three blocks from Paul's jail cell, but it might as well have been three hundred miles.

As if she needed a reminder of the situation, the morning paper on her coffee table contained a small front page article with a headline that blared out "HALCYON FURY." The article described the critical injury of Ronald Withers on the *Halcyon* and the arrest of Paul Tyson with an alleged motive for assault, and concluded by pointing out that the meaning of the word halcyon, ironically, is peaceful.

Finally realizing it was time to fix something to eat for dinner, Joan paused once more at her window and looked out across the U.S. 31 Shore Drive at the slow gray drizzle dimpling the calm surface of West Arm. She turned toward the fridge with no enthusiasm. She vacillated between believing that Paul would not have assaulted Ron so viciously, and fearing that he had done so. Images of Paul smashing a two-by-four into Ron's head flashed into her thoughts. Having no idea how long this agony would go on, Joan began to realize that learning the truth had become more important than anything else in her life right now.

Joan pulled some leftover spaghetti out of the fridge. She poured herself a glass of pinot noir, spilling a bunch of it with her shaky grip on the bottle. She pushed the spaghetti around on her plate and gulped the wine. She poured another glass, using both hands this time. *Jesus Christ.* She decided to call one of the students she knew pretty well who was on the *Halcyon* yesterday.

"Bonnie, it's Joan Brockton."

"Oh, hi."

"What do you know about the accident yesterday?" Joan was determined to talk about it as an accident.

"Joan, I'm not supposed to talk about it"

"I guess I should have known that. I just wish there was some way to find out if anyone knew where Paul Tyson was the whole time."

"So do I Joan, but I just can't help with that. I'm sorry."

"That's okay, Bonnie. Sorry to bother you."

Joan ended the call and dropped the idea of calling every student who may have been on the cruise. She stared back out at the gray bay for a while, tried watching some of a PBS show on TV, and finally went to bed.

# CHAPTER
# 11

On Monday, June 14, the weather was sunny and warm. Joan and Dr. Perry had received calls from Craig Basham saying that Paul's arraignment was scheduled for one p.m. today in Courtroom C in the courthouse. Joan spent the morning at the institute getting some work done. Joan found that she welcomed the distraction of doing some routine chores in the lab. She caught up on glassware washing, disposed of some recent electrophoresis gels in the hazardous waste, ordered more micropipette tips, and so on. *I should have been in here yesterday, instead of stewing around in my apartment all day. How stupid.*

At noon, Dr. Perry came by Joan's lab and suggested that they get some lunch on the way to the courthouse. They drove in Dr. Perry's car several blocks east on U.S. 31. Tourist traffic was light in this early part of the season. After a quick burger, they headed back west to the courthouse.

They found their way to Courtroom C, richly wood-paneled and currently very quiet. Paul was seated at the defendant's table, wearing a black blazer, a blue Nautica shirt, and khakis. *Basham must have picked up the court-worthy clothes from Paul's boat,* Joan thought. Craig Basham was dressed in a lawyerly gray suit and maroon tie, and was talking quietly with the prosecutor and the judge up at the bench. The marine division inspector was seated at the prosecutor's table. Dr. Bates was present, seated over on the right side of the spectator gallery with some people who obviously were Ron Withers' parents and sister. Withers' mother was smoldering in tears. Paul's mother was no longer living, and his father was overseas on business and unable to get back yet for this rather sudden situation. Joan and Dr. Perry joined RULI director Dr. Tollefson on the left side of the gallery and waited for things to get started.

At one p.m. sharp, the bailiff announced the arraignment. Craig Basham sat down beside Paul, and the judge invited the prosecutor to proceed. The prosecutor stated the charge of assault with intent to do great bodily harm and described the motive on the basis of Paul Tyson's violent threat to Ronald Withers witnessed by many people in Ann Arbor, as well as his anger at Withers upon boarding the ship on Saturday, also witnessed by several people, all of which had been learned by the marine division investigator during his interrogation of the students on the ship.

The opportunity to commit this crime was provided by Tyson being on the ship with Withers during the cruise, with no accounting of Tyson's location during the time that Withers was reported missing. The prosecutor also requested that Mr. Tyson be held without bail because of the extremely critical condition of the victim. Withers' mother sobbed audibly.

The judge asked the prosecutor if there was any direct evidence that the defendant had assaulted Mr. Withers, such as witnesses and/or a weapon traceable to the defendant. The prosecutor said that there was none yet, but that the investigation was continuing. He said no more. He did not care to elaborate on the fact that, so far, there was no one who had said that they had seen Paul assault Ron or even seen Paul anywhere near him on the ship. And the forensic team had not yet found anything resembling an appropriate weapon that could be tied physically, that is by DNA-laden material and fingerprints, to both Ron and Paul. But the forensic team was working around the clock while the ship remained plastered with yellow crime scene tape and guarded by pacing deputies. The search image they had in mind was something of the size and heft of a baseball bat with Paul's fingerprints on the handle and Ron's DNA on the barrel.

The judge asked Paul to rise. "Mr. Tyson, how do you plead?"

Paul cleared his throat. "Not guilty, your honor." He stared at the judge until he was asked to be seated.

Paul's attorney Craig Basham then stood and asked that Paul be released pending grand jury proceedings. He cited Paul's impeccable reputation, lack of prior criminal record, and his productive association with the institute right here in town. The judge was silent for a few minutes while reading over the printed version of the case.

Then the judge said, "The defendant will be released on fifty thousand dollars bond, and is directed to remain in the area pending the ongoing investigation and the grand jury process."

The prosecutor rose and objected, asking at least for a far higher bail figure, preferably ten times higher, but the judge held firm. He reminded the prosecutor of the lack of direct evidence against the defendant and added that he assumed that the institute could be relied on to cooperate in keeping Mr. Tyson available. The judge looked out at Dr. Tollefson, who gave a quick nod. The gavel came down, and the bailiff dismissed the courtroom.

Paul did not look at the unhappy Withers family as he and Craig Basham walked up the aisle to join Joan and Dr. Perry. Perry shook Paul's hand, and Joan hugged him briefly, saying, "Let's get out of here!"

"Well, not so fast. We have to arrange Paul's bail first," said Craig. "Tell you what, Paul and I will go do that, and then meet you two at my house for a beer. It's just a few blocks from here." Craig gave Joan and Dr. Perry the address, and led Paul out toward the courthouse offices. Craig had brought Paul's title to *Tondeleyo* along with Paul's clothes that morning, and he expected that they would have little problem securing the fifty thousand dollar bond.

Driving a few blocks south, Dr. Perry and Joan pulled up and parked in front of Craig Basham's handsome Victorian house. It was on a shady street in the middle of Traverse City's signature neighborhood of mansions and sumptuous cottages built with the fortunes and pine boards amassed by the lumber barons in the late nineteenth century. Those barons were long gone, and thankfully the once denuded forests of northern Michigan were again resplendent in mature second growth, now supporting tourism as the primary economy base. But those old houses, over a dozen leafy blocks of them, had all been restored by now, and stood in stately grandeur. In the light breeze, a shifting mosaic of leaf shadows played on the sun dappled lawn. The continuous *breeee* of cicadas droned somewhere in the foliage.

"I was pleased to hear the Judge emphasize the rather thin case they have," remarked Perry.

"Well yeah, me too," replied Joan. "But no one seems to think it could have been an accident. If not, who would have hit Ron. You and Craig probably know Paul better than I do. I just can't shake a nagging fear that he actually could have done this. Tell me I'm wrong, Dr. Perry."

"I know how you feel, but I have to believe you're wrong. There has to be another explanation."

They waited a while longer in silence. Finally Craig pulled into his driveway, and he and Paul got out of the Ford Escape hybrid. Joan and Dr. Perry got out of Perry's car and joined them in the front yard.

"These houses are magnificent," said Perry, staring up at Craig's pale lavender gingerbread porch. "Painted Ladies, I guess they call them."

"Thanks, yes they are," replied Craig, loosening his tie. "Except for those goofy three foot wide metal strips they installed along all the roof edges. Most of these houses have them, supposedly something to do with winter ice protection, but I don't know if they really do much, and they sure look out of place on these old gals. Sort of a fad that swept through town some years ago, I guess. Well, let's go in. I'll show you the house, and we can sit out on the back deck. I phoned my wife at her office and warned her there might be a bit of a crowd here when she gets home." Craig took off his suit jacket and led them toward his front door.

After the brief house tour, they filed out the back door with cold cans of Dos Equis, and settled into deck chairs. "So welcome back Mr. Tyson," said Dr. Perry. "I assume it's good to get out of that place."

With his feet crossed, Paul swirled his beer can slowly, and nodded. He seemed to have aged ten years, and right now he looked like a middle aged professor in a three hour committee meeting. He managed a thin smile.

"You have no idea." Paul then looked over at his attorney. "Craig, thanks, my friend. So far so good, I guess."

"Well, you can thank the fact that their case is so thin," replied Basham. "Let's hope it stays that way, and that we come up with something to make it even thinner."

Paul nodded slowly again, but had no more to say. Joan stared down at the deck boards, twisting her beer can in her rigid hands.

"Paul, before the cruise you mentioned something to me about wanting to throw Ron off the fantail. I just have to know...." She couldn't get the rest of it out.

Paul knew what she was trying to ask him. Instantly red in the face, he stood up, clenched his fists, and threw his crumpled beer can to the deck with a bang that nearly sent Dr. Perry over backwards in his chair. "Now you too, Joan? You didn't hear me in court today?" asked Paul. "I don't need this shit," he said as he strode off around toward the front of the house.

Craig started to follow Paul. "Paul, can I drive you?"

"No, I'd rather walk. It's not that far to my car at the institute." Paul disappeared down the driveway.

Craig returned to the deck to find Joan trembling in tears. "Look Joan, you need to understand that Paul does not like that question coming from anybody. Stubborn pride, I guess. I hope. And on top of all this, he had to defend himself against a pair of mean drunks in jail on Saturday night. One of them is in the hospital now."

"My god. Did you know he could be so violent?"

"No. Except for a fight he had in a high school football game he once told me about, I never saw him lose it or get violent in all of our college days together."

Dr. Perry added, "During his years here, Paul has always been even-tempered and rock steady. He's the seniormost grad student at RULI, and they call him 'the grownup.'"

"But everyone has his breaking point," said Craig. "Um...Joan, did he really say that about the fantail?"

"Yes."

"Well, that would be gasoline on a bonfire to a jury. In any case, right now the most important question for me is not, did he assault Withers, but can they convict him of it. I'm hoping they can't even indict him."

"So in your world, 'Not guilty your honor' means 'You won't get me for this,' doesn't it?" Joan said.

"Sometimes."

"And this time?"

"As far as I know right now, no one other than Paul knows that for sure," replied Craig. "But as I said, the law operates the same either way."

"That's hardly comforting to me. As a scientist, I have a huge problem with the rules of evidence in law, despite their intended protection of the rights of the accused. I want to know the truth, not the filtered story a jury is instructed to consider."

"I understand, believe me," said Craig. "But remember, the rules of law also protect *innocent* people from unfair tactics of prosecutors. So hang in there. We'll get to the truth."

Joan calmed down a bit. But she wasn't quite finished.

"Craig, forgive me, but what kind of lawyer are you exactly? Someone said..."

"Yes," Craig interrupted. "I am not a criminal lawyer. The best I can say is that I have litigated a whole bunch of court cases in environmental lawsuits, some very nasty ones. My record speaks for itself, but I'm the first to admit that I am not real comfortable here. Paul pushed me hard to take this case. I insisted that I get appropriate help if and when needed. That's our deal."

Joan nodded, but still looked troubled.

"Well, I wish you the best, and I do thank you for your efforts." Joan stood up. "Dr. Perry, can we go now? I think this party is over."

Perry stood and said, "Sure Joan. Craig, I thank you too, and I hope that soon we can do this again with more to be happy about."

"You got it," said Basham.

As Joan and Dr. Perry went around to her truck, Craig began collecting empty cans and wondering how much of a mistake Paul was making using Craig for his defense. He began going through a mental list of the criminal defense attorneys he knew. *Better get one of 'em throwing in the bull pen.*

# Chapter

## *12*

Tuesday morning, June 15, was already sunny and warm again when Paul pulled his Mustang into the institute lot. He had driven home to his boat yesterday, gotten a sandwich, and polished off a six pack of Corona before dropping into his first night's sleep since Friday.

He entered the limnology building and went straight into the Perry lab to begin work on his next set of lab experiments on pH and temperature optima of algal species he had isolated and cultured from Lake Michigan. He worked at keeping Joan from coming to mind, but failed over and over. Nevertheless, he stayed where he was and worked all the harder on his research.

Dr. Perry came by the lab around eleven, and asked Paul if he still wanted to write up the plagiarism charge to be submitted to Director Tollefson. Paul said, "Yep," and they walked down the hall to Perry's office.

Dr. Perry said, "I don't know how this is going to play under the circumstances." Paul knew he was talking about the propriety of bringing charges against a man who was lying near death with a broken head.

"I can't help that. We need to get this cleared up so we can publish my data," replied Paul.

"Okay, well, what we can use now is printouts of your graphed data files that match those they used, a copy of their paper, and the affidavits I got this morning from Sara and Mahmoud stating that they assisted in those experiments in our lab. Your raw data notebooks would be better, but I assume those are still missing."

"Yes, they are. But I'll go print those graphs right now," said Paul, and he went back to the lab.

After lunch, Paul returned to the lab, and Dr. Perry took the documents to RULI Director Dr. Karen Tollefson's office.

"Come on in James. Well, we've seen better days. What have you got?"

"Here is the plagiarism charge, with supporting documents," said Perry. "The case would be stronger with Paul's original notebooks, but as you know, they were stolen."

"You're not specifically charging them with the notebook theft, are you?"

"No, no. That would be unsupportable as of now."

"Jim, it's hard to prove a negative; what I mean is, that they didn't do the same experiments themselves. Couldn't they have done that?"

"Not impossible, but highly unlikely. They have no background for that, and they don't have the right equipment or even the algal cultures Paul used."

"Well, okay. Anyway, I'm afraid I'm going to have to sit on this at least for a while, until Ron's condition resolves, hopefully by coming out of that coma and getting better. I just can't lay this on him and his family right now."

"I'm not surprised, Karen, and I don't blame you."

"And then there's this other problem: It would seem that the stronger the case for the plagiarism, the stronger the case for the motive to assault Ron. Isn't Paul worried about that?"

Dr. Perry paused for a moment. "Well *I* am, to tell the truth, but I don't think he is. His sense of pride in all of this is immense."

"Jim, what do you think about the assault charge?"

"None of us knows very much about what happened Saturday on *Halcyon*," replied Perry. "But look: *I* can't believe that Paul assaulted Ron. Yes Paul got a little hot in Ann Arbor...okay he got very hot. But he is no beast. Students don't try to kill each other over plagiarism. Sure, now and then a deranged student goes berserk and kills people on a campus, but no way is Paul remotely in that category."

"I tend to agree, Jim. I surely hope that something breaks that clears it all up. I hope that poor Ron Withers wakes up and says it was an accident. Of course I hope he wakes up no matter what happened. But we're told there is no change today. By the way, do you have any idea the kind of lawsuit we will face no matter what happens from now on?"

"I hate to even try to imagine it," Perry replied. "Well I'll get back to the grind. Thanks a lot, Karen." Dr. Perry rose and started back to his office. On the way, he stopped by the lab and told Paul that Dr. Tollefson had received the plagiarism charge, but that she intended to postpone filing it with the provost for a while.

"Figures," said Paul.

"She has to do what she has to do, Paul. It will get filed. Let's worry about you, and about Ron's health right now."

"Amen to that."

"Are you able to get anything worthwhile done in the lab at this point?" asked Perry.

"Well, it's a struggle, but I did accomplish some things this morning. I think I'll be okay for the time being."

"Okay. Let me know what I can do. You know we are with you on this thing."

"Thanks, Dr. Perry."

Perry shambled out of the lab toward his office. Paul drew a deep breath and turned back to his space on the lab bench. Exhaling slowly through pursed lips, he methodically began weighing out reagents to mix new nutrient stocks for his algal culture media. Starting with the potassium phosphate, he worked his way through the dozen or so compounds that he used to simulate Lake Michigan water chemistry. The late afternoon sun glared through the lab windows by the time he finished the last reagent stock. Thoughts of Joan loomed as he tidied up the lab and headed out for his car. The drive to Elk Rapids would not be pleasant.

On into the week, Paul immersed himself in his lab work, each day making a surprising amount of progress. But during the evenings aboard *Tondeleyo* he was unable to avoid thinking about what the Ron Withers situation had done to his life, and about losing touch with Joan. And he made no progress in resolving any of those thoughts.

Paul cooked simple meals or ate up in town with no enthusiasm. He tried to read his paperback books from the library. The stories did not make much of an impression; he would probably be able to re-read them later and think they were new.

Ron Withers remained comatose on life support.

# Chapter 13

During that same week, Joan did not fare so well in the lab. She had taken to coming very early in the morning and leaving late at night to avoid running into Paul in the parking lot. Her advisor's lab was in the biology building, which was next to the limnology building where the Perry lab was. She brought a bag lunch so that once inside there was little chance of seeing Paul during the day. But avoiding him did not make her feel any better.

She kept making stupid mistakes every day. Twice she ruined PCR runs by programming the thermocycler incorrectly. She overran electrophoresis runs. She made pipetting errors while making up stock reagents. Wednesday was a little better when she took a drive south on 31 to the Platte River state hatchery near Beulah to pick up some more Coho fingerlings. And that evening she worked off some tension with a good long run along the bay. But Thursday she dropped and broke a bottle of acid, which brought in the hazmat people, and by late that Friday afternoon it had fully dawned on her. *What a damn mess I am. This is nuts.*

Just then, Larry Griffin stuck his head in the door of her lab and said, "Hey Joan."

"Hey Larry," she said back to him, wondering what he was doing here. Larry Griffin was a first year grad student at the institute, a nice looking kid who was rotating in several different labs like all first year grads did. Joan's lab was not one of them, and she did not know him very well.

"Got that Coho genome all worked out?" Griffin asked.
"Don't I wish. What's on your mind?"
"Thought you might want to go get a beer."

*So I'm the wounded quail, attracting the bird dogs now*, she thought. *Might want to go get a beer, eh? Hell yes, I want to go get a beer.* "You're on, Larry. Let me shut things down here. I'll meet you in the parking lot in ten minutes."

Paul was leaving the lab himself about then, and stopped short when he opened the door of the limno building and saw Joan getting in Larry Griffin's car. Paul waited for them to drive out of the parking lot before going to his Mustang. He stared long and hard at Griffin's car as it headed into town. He started his Mustang, gunned it loudly and jammed it into first gear. He burned rubber all the way out of the parking lot and onto U.S. 31. He caught rubber in all the rest of the gears and leveled off at a speed that risked a speeding ticket all the way to Elk Rapids.

It was crowded and noisy in the brew pub, but the draft pints were going down very smoothly. Joan felt better than she had for over a week, though she was glad she didn't have to make a lot of small talk in all that racket. It was enough just to be slamming suds like an undergrad with a cute guy. Things were getting a little fuzzy, but Larry's longish black hair and dark eyes were still a pretty decent distraction from the funk she was in. Somewhere in there they had some burgers and fries.

Shortly after eleven o'clock they drove back to her Blazer in the institute lot. Standing by her door, Griffin leaned over and gave Joan a kiss. She didn't return it, but she didn't turn away from it.

"Dinner tomorrow?" asked Larry.
*Oh shit. Oh what the hell.* "Yeah, that would be nice."
"Pick you up at seven. Where do you live?"
Joan told him the address, and got in her truck.

The next morning Joan was a little hungover, but she went in to the lab anyway. She didn't want to stew around all day at home waiting for this damn second "date" she had agreed to while she was fog-headed last night. By early afternoon she felt pretty good, and she actually had her best day all week at the bench and got some stuff done without screwing anything up. She wanted to call Larry and call off the dinner thing, but she did not have his unlisted number. So she went home at five-thirty to get ready.

Dinner at the waterfront restaurant on West Bay Shore Drive was excellent, with a pleasant view of the bay from the deck. When Griffin insisted on picking up the pricey tab, Joan warned herself *this is a very old ploy*. But she agreed to his suggestion that they drive over to a country western tavern on Traverse Highway.

Joan actually liked country music, and she got caught up in the fun. They did a lot of line dancing, and paraded around the floor in the couples dances. The place looked like a roller rink with cowboy boots in place of skates. They sang at the top of their lungs through "Sweet Home Alabama," "The Oasis," and all the other classics. They made countless new lifelong friends they would never see again. And they drank countless bottles of beer that were barely cold as demand outpaced the supply in the refrigerators. By midnight Joan was tanked and exhausted.

"Take me home, cowboy."

"Yes ma'm."

They returned to town along Bay Shore Drive where it joined U.S. 31 north. Griffin slowed his car and asked Joan if she would like to go up to the end of Mission Point. The beach beyond the old lighthouse there is beautiful at night.

"Um...no. Just head on back to my place, okay? I'm really tired."

"You're the boss," Griffin replied.

At Joan's door, she fumbled with her key. Griffin gently took it from her hand and opened the door. He gave her a dose of his bedroom eyes and steered her into the apartment. He turned on the TV and tuned it to Saturday Night Live, and said, "Lets watch this a while." Joan nodded, and they sat back on the only place to do that in that one-room apartment: her daybed with the large bolsters along the wall.

They watched for a while, and Joan realized they were holding hands. Then Griffin slid his hand part way up her thigh. "I've got a long drive. How 'bout I stay here for the night?"

Joan fought back out of her beer haze. "I don't think so. Can you go now? I've got to get to sleep."

"C'mon sweetie, let's celebrate this nice evening. You won't regret it."

"No, Larry, really."

"Well, would it help my case if I said I would tell the authorities that I know that Paul Tyson was on the boat deck the whole time?"

Joan came fully alert. "You WHAT? You were on *Halcyon* that day? What are you talking about?"

"I'm saying maybe I can get Tyson's case dismissed."

"*Did* you see him up there the whole time?"

"No, but I'm pretty sure Dr. Bates did. He was in his room the whole time working on a proposal, and he could see Paul from his aft window."

"How do you know?"

"Because I was in there for a while helping him with the proposal. So how 'bout it? I spend the night, you get me off, and I get Paul off, so to speak."

Joan stood up. "That's totally disgusting. Would you please go now?"

But it was obvious that Larry's sex drive was in high gear now.

"Let's put it this way missy. You don't come across here, I tell the prosecution that I saw Tyson go below when Ron did. He'll be toast."

Joan crossed the room and yanked open the door.

"GET OUT OF HERE. NOW."

Joan pulled Griffin toward the door, hoping like hell that a full-fledged rape attempt wasn't coming next. But Griffin did allow himself to be pushed on out the door. He turned and said, "Well, guess I'll make an appointment with that prosecutor."

Joan slammed the door, engaged the chain lock, and leaned her head against the door. Eyes closed, she gasped for breath for several minutes. Then she walked on shaky legs to the bathroom and threw up half the beer that she had swilled that evening. She stumbled back out and over to her bed, where she collapsed and fell asleep with her clothes on.

# CHAPTER 14

The next morning, Joan did not wake up until noon. Her head pounded like her brain was trying to escape through her eyes, and her mouth felt like there was an old wool sock in there. She got up and ate some cold cereal and milk, about the only thing she could stomach. She got out of last night's clothes and took a long shower. The hot water felt good, but it didn't make her feel any less stupid about getting involved with that asshole Griffin. She dried off and pulled on some jeans and a tee shirt and lay back down on her bed.

Even with her eyes shut tight, Joan kept seeing a looping video of last night's events, round and round from the out-of-control cowboy bar fun to the dangerous assault in her apartment, again and again. Finally she got up and shook her head. That was a bad idea. It took five minutes for the dizzy throbbing to subside.

After some Tylenol and another half hour lying down, it finally dawned on Joan. *I've got to call Craig Basham.* She got up and looked in the phone book. Surprisingly, Craig Basham's home number was listed there. Small town lawyer. She dialed it.

"Craig, this is Joan Brockton."

"Hello Joan. What's up? You don't sound so good."

"Well, as a matter of fact, my relationship with Paul currently involves a certain amount of conflict, in the same sense that Lake Michigan involves a certain amount of water. That's a paraphrase of Dave Barry."

"Who is Dave Barry?"

"You know, that guy that writes all those hilarious satire books."

"Oh yeah, that Dave Barry."

"Anyway, that's not why I called, exactly. Craig, I learned something that could be really important from Larry Griffin last night. You don't want to know how I happened to learn it."

"Who is Larry Griffin?"

"A student who was on the *Halcyon* that day. Now listen Craig, he told me that Dr. Bates was in his cabin the whole time, and he could see Paul on the boat deck from his porthole. If Paul was up there the whole time, Bates may know that."

"That's very interesting."

"Yes, but there is a complication. Things got ugly last night, and Griffin threatened to tell the prosecutor that he saw Paul go below. It would be a lie, but a very damaging one."

"Shit," said Craig. "Well, it would be shaky, coming this late, but nonetheless we sure don't need that. But I will pursue the Bates angle, see if there is some way we can learn what he knows. He certainly hasn't said anything about personal knowledge of Paul's whereabouts, but he is clearly not in Paul's corner in this thing. Joan, take care of yourself. We are going to get through this. Trust me."

"Craig, thanks. I promise I will get a grip."

About an hour after her call to Craig, Joan wasn't getting much of a grip. Some of last night's country music was rattling around in her mind, and she decided to put on an old Patty Loveless CD. Might as well wallow in those tear jerkin' tunes of one of her favorite country singers. But when the *Only What I Feel* album got to the fourth cut, it was a little too much – Patty was singing about two estranged lovers sitting by their phones waiting for a call from each other.

Those words were landing like cannon balls right in Joan's wheelhouse. The song went on, and during the third repeat of the chorus, Joan's phone rang. Her heart leapt up into her throat. She switched off the stereo and picked up the phone receiver.

"Joan?" It was not Paul's voice.

She was silent for a moment. "Who is this?"

"Dave Washington." It was the RULI marine operations superintendent. "Joan, I'm sorry to call you on a Sunday, but we have an urgent situation here." Now Joan was panicking. *What has happened? Did Paul do something...?*

"What is it," she managed in a small voice.

"Last night the *Halcyon* was cleared. The forensic investigation has been completed, and we can continue now with the cruises. We're already a week behind schedule, and Dr. Tollefson wants us to get back on schedule as quickly as possible. A lot of grant money is riding on it. So anyway, we are sailing tomorrow on the benthos cruise, and we need hands. Can you sail on this short notice?"

Joan's heart dropped back down out of her throat and slowed down. "Um...yeah, I guess I can do that. What time, the usual seven-thirty a.m.?"

"Yep."

"Dave, will Paul Tyson be aboard?"

"No, he is not allowed anywhere near *Halcyon*."

"Did they find anything?"

"Who?"

"The forensic guys."

"I don't know yet."

"Well, okay. Oh, but one more question. Will Larry Griffin be on the cruise?"

"Let me look at the roster," said Washington. "No, he won't. Why?"

"Never mind. I'll be there at oh seven hundred."

"Thanks a bunch, Joan"

With a new thing to focus on, Joan got something more to eat, and then began packing for a week's cruise. This would probably be just what she needed right now.

# CHAPTER 15

On Monday morning *Halcyon* was ready to sail, and Joan was feeling pretty good in the breezy sunshine; it was nice just to be aboard a boat again. She was on the fantail with the other student techs, and she thanked the gods that neither Paul nor Larry Griffin was among them. As the *Halcyon* backed around to leave the harbor, Joan glanced back ashore and saw Paul leaning against the wall near the door of the limno building, watching them depart.

*Halcyon's* departure slowly widened the distance between them, and her tenuous bit of cheer vanished. Still she looked, and found herself raising her hand in a small, tentative wave. Paul watched her for a couple of beats, and then he did the same thing. He turned for the door, and she turned to walk forward along the port side deck.

Just then, a clamor arose as four undergrad coeds came running down the jetty, shrieking and waving. Four of the male students whistled and returned the waves. They whooped and waved until *Halcyon* was out of earshot. Joan couldn't help grinning at all the fuss. *Those undergrad hormones are all in perfect working order, and raging as usual.* She turned and walked toward the bow in the bracing headwind as *Halcyon* steamed northward up the bay.

Joan found three other students perched on the mooring bits and sampling equipment along the starboard bow rail, all of them staring intently at their smartphone screens.

"Aren't we a flock of seagulls, eh?" said Joan.

"What do you mean?" replied one of the students.

"Oh, you haven't heard any of the ship's crew call us seagulls?"

Joan explained that professional commercial sailors often refer to any non-working passengers as seagulls, referring to the way that seagulls and other seabirds sometimes alight on deck and just sit around for awhile, passengers being equally useless to the ship's work, and just as much of a nuisance.

"But we are scientific workers, and that's the point of the ship and the cruises," said one of the other students.

"Yes, but a lot of ship's crew members don't really get that point. They're not accustomed to research vessels, and they just get annoyed when we stop for sampling stations and delay the voyage to the next port. To them the ship is supposed to get from port A to port B as fast as possible. So we're a nuisance to them. But those guys are very good at what they do, and we respect them for that and ignore the seagull crap, so to speak."

This conversation was distracting Joan a bit now from the Larry Griffin episode. Joan looked up and caught the eye of the young helmsman in the pilothouse. She flapped her elbows like a bird, and he grinned and waved at her. The other student "seagulls" waved back at him, and then resumed texting each other on their smartphones. Joan sat back and relaxed as the *Halcyon* plowed ahead.

Back in the limnology building, Paul went to the Perry lab and got to work. He was doing some sterile transfers of algal cultures to fresh agar slants, when the phone rang. It was Craig Basham.

"Paul, two things. First, just an update that Ron Withers remains comatose. Second, I have learned that Dr. Bates was in his cabin all that morning."

"So?"

"He could see you on the boat deck from his aft porthole while he was working on his computer, and presumably would know if and when you changed location"

Paul was silent for a moment. "How did you learn that?"

"A little birdie told me."

"Come on, Craig. Don't bullshit me. I got enough people doing that."

"Okay. Joan told me."

"How does she know? And no more little birdies."

"She was told this by Larry Griffin. Seems he was aboard that morning, and was with Bates part of the time. Not the whole time, but he said Bates was there the whole time."

"Craig, I saw Joan leaving campus with Griffin on Friday. Am I losing her to that twit? What in billy-hell is going on?"

"Well, if you are losing her, I doubt if it's to that twit. Apparently things went sour, and he threatened to tell the prosecution he saw you go below that morning. Untrue, but I get the impression the threat was supposed to get him some leverage with her."

"Fucking hell. The bastard is just down the hall here. He's rotating in Bates' lab, for Christ sake."

"Paul, don't you dare go near him. In fact when we get off the phone, I want you to go back to your boat and stay there for a week. Will you do that?"

"Yeah. I'll go."

"Good. Now I need to get a deposition from Bates under oath. Who should I talk to first?"

"I'd suggest Dr. Karen Tollefson, our director here. Captain Robado too, but he just took *Halcyon* out for the week. Joan is on the cruise, by the way."

"Probably a good place for her right now. Okay, I'll get on the Bates thing. Now get your sorry ass out of there. I want to get a call from you in half an hour, and I want to hear *Tondeleyo's* halyards clanking next to you."

"I'm on my way. Thanks again buddy."

Out on the *Halcyon,* everyone got set up for the day's series of sampling stations, at which they would be taking bottom sediment samples. The big dangerous contraption know as the Smith-McIntyre dredge was unlashed from its deck housing and shackled to the winch cable beside the hero board, the steel grated deck extension on which a technician deployed and retrieved over-the-side equipment. A field notebook was prepared with the date and the list of sampling stations. A sediment screening apparatus was set up, and two boxes of sample jars were prepared, one set for raw unscreened sediment for the geologists and one set for the benthic animals screened out of the sediment for the biologists.

After everything was ready, the scientific crew sat around on deck with time to relax for a while in the sun until they reached the first station. It was not entirely pleasant, however. The wind had died away to nothing, and a swarm of biting flies descended out of nowhere like they always did whenever it was dead calm and warm, even out there in the middle of Lake Michigan. Everyone swatted and swore, but it was too nice to sit around inside.

At about eleven a.m., *Halcyon* slowed and stopped for the first sampling station. A couple of the guys used a crowbar to cock the steel spring-loaded jaws in the open position, ready for the messenger weight to trip them shut on the lake bottom.

"That thing looks dangerous," Joan remarked.

"Yeah," said one of the two guys. To the other student tech, he said, "You ever try to deploy this thing when there are waves rolling the ship?"

"Yeah, it's lethal then. You got to fend it off with your foot while it is swinging into the hero board, before it is submerged. Get it wrong, and the bastard takes a bite of your foot. The whole thing weighs about fifty pounds, and those springs must have a hundred pounds of pressure."

"Got that right. And if a wave hits it just right going in, it trips by itself, and you have to haul it back aboard and cock it again. Had to do that two or three times at each station, one day last summer. Nice to have a real calm day today."

Today the dredge went under the calm surface smoothly. When it reached the bottom, the guy on the hero board sent the messenger weight down the cable, and the sampler came up full of bottom sediment. One jar was filled with raw sample, and the rest of the sample was put in the screener and hosed down. Joan held the data notebook, and squinted in bright sun as she wrote down the descriptive comments dictated by one of the geology students.

"Sample One-A. LS. Two more samples to go at this station."

"What is LS?" asked Joan.

"Loon shit," replied the student.

"Really?" It was dark brown and gooey.

"Really. Go ahead and taste it."

Joan said, "You taste it, smart-ass."

So the kid scooped some with his finger a tasted it. "Yep. Loon shit."

Joan made a face. "You're nuts."

"Okay, it's really just very fine silt with lots of organic matter. It was given the "loon shit" label by some creative students years ago, and the code name stuck, probably because it's easy to write down in the book. The tasting trick is Dr. Hugle's prank on all the new students. Some of 'em actually do it." Dr. Hugle was the geologist who was the chief scientist on this cruise.

Joan laughed and filled in the box on the form. "LS it is."

The benthos sampling routine went on, station after station, crisscrossing Lake Michigan day after day through most of the week with very pleasant weather. Joan enjoyed the routine, and was happy not to have to struggle with her own research for a while. Each night the *Halcyon* put in to a port either in Michigan or Wisconsin. Each night the scientific crew and some of the ship's crew hit the nearest bars. The *Halcyon* did not dock at fancy marinas, but at commercial docks, and the shot-and-beer bars in those districts were pretty rough. But the draft beer was cheap. Joan and the more senior staff and officers kept it to just a couple each night, but there was no such restraint among most of the undergrads and young deckhands. Those poor sods had splitting headaches every morning, and by ten a.m. they would swear they were staying aboard tonight. But by five p.m. they were at the rail ready to hit the bars again. Joan shook her head, but said nothing. *Can't say I was any less foolish last weekend.*

# CHAPTER 16

On Wednesday, June 23, Craig Basham drove to the institute for his two p.m. appointment to depose Dr. Bates. Craig found that Bates was already in the director's conference room on the second floor of the limnology building. Bates was sipping a Styrofoam cup of coffee, and he frowned darkly when Craig entered the room. Craig poured himself a coffee from the sideboard and sat down across the table from Dr. Bates.

"Dr. Bates, I appreciate your meeting with me today. I only have a few questions for you. I'm going to turn on this tape recorder, which is standard practice for depositions. Is that agreeable to you?"

Bates frowned again, but said, "Yes, go ahead."

Basham started the recorder and said, "Please state your name and today's date."

Bates did so.

"I am Craig Basham, defense attorney for Mr. Paul Tyson. Dr. Bates, please state that you understand that you are under oath to speak the truth as if in a court of law."

"I understand."

Craig first asked Bates to summarize his memory of the events on the Saturday of Ron Withers' injury aboard the *Halcyon*. Bates did so, and Craig learned nothing new. Craig then asked him his first question.

"It has come to my attention that you were in your chief scientist's stateroom the entire time the ship was underway, until Ron Griffin was reported missing. Is that true?"

Bates hesitated. "Yes"

"Could you see Paul Tyson from your window?"

Bates hesitated again. "Yes."

"Was Tyson there on the deck the whole time?"

Bates stared silently and chipped off small pieces of Styrofoam from his empty coffee cup with his thumbnail.

"I don't know," Bates finally replied.

"Are you sure?"

Bates hesitated again. "Yes, I don't know."

Craig was tempted to reveal the fact that Larry Griffin had threatened Joan that he would claim that he saw Paul follow Withers below. Maybe he could catch Bates off guard and he would contradict Griffin. But Craig decided that was probably not a good idea; too risky.

"Dr. Bates, thank you for your cooperation. That is all for now."

Craig turned off the recorder, packed it up, and left the room. It had probably been a waste of time, but it had to be done. And just maybe he had some perjury there on the tape. *You never know*, thought Craig as he exited the building.

# Chapter 17

On Friday, June 25, the week's fine weather deteriorated somewhat on northern Lake Michigan, and the wind picked up. By mid morning it was blowing about fifteen knots and gusting to twenty, and the research crew had to work while *Halcyon* lay rolling in the trough. Joan watched the poor guys struggling with that damn "bear trap" bottom sampler on the hero board. They were now at the third station of the day.

After finally getting the dredge under the surface without tripping it and then lowering it to the bottom, the kid on the hero board fumbled the messenger weight and lost it over the side. "Goddamn it. That's the last one we have on deck," he said.

The chief scientist turned to Joan. "Would you go down in the storage hold and see if there are any extra messenger weights among that stuff? You'll have to get Captain Robado to go with you; he has it locked, and keeps the key with him. Tell him we can't finish the stations without one."

"Okay, sure."

Joan actually was not at all sure she wanted to go into that awful hold where Ron Withers was found, but damned if she was going to be a wimp about it. She went forward to find the Captain.

In the storage room below, Robado knelt down and unlocked the padlock on the hatch to the hold. He lifted the hatch and swung it back on its retainer chain. With a flashlight, Joan stepped down inside. The life jackets that Ron Withers had bled on were gone, and there was nothing to show that a tragedy had happened here. Joan started rummaging around in the stuff nearest to her, looking for spare messenger weights. Finding none at first, she bent down below the edge of the hatch opening and crawled forward on hands and knees through piles of various equipment. Finally she uncovered one messenger weight. Reaching to grab it, her hand brushed against two notebooks that were lying partway out of a canvas backpack. They were standard lab notebooks. She started to back up with the messenger weight, and then she froze.

Paul was missing two lab notebooks. Her heart tripped over itself and then raced. Still holding the messenger weight, she grabbed the books and scrambled backward into the open area. The flashlight helped reveal the name on the covers of both notebooks. Paul Tyson. With trembling hands, Joan flipped through them and saw handwritten data entries on phytoplankton productivity.

"CAPTAIN. These are Paul Tyson's missing lab notebooks. Jesus Christ."

Just then *Halcyon* took a more violent roll to port. Joan lost her balance and dropped one of the books. She bent down to pick it up and as she started to straighten up, the ship rolled strongly back to starboard, and BLAM.

The hatch slammed shut with so much force that the noise and pressure stunned her and she fell flat in the darkness. Her ears were ringing as Captain Robado pulled the hatch back open and said, "Are you okay, did it hit you?"

She could hardly hear him. He asked her again more loudly, and she shook her head.

"It didn't hit me, but if I had risen up a second sooner it would have. It could have killed me. Oh…my…god…, CAPTAIN. That's what must have happened to Ron. Was it rough that day? Sure it was. It was a horrible accident. Oh my god, it was all a horrible accident." She felt light headed. She felt light all over.

Robado thought a minute. "Well if Withers stole those lab books like Paul says he did, then that could explain why Ron was down here in this hold that morning. Come on up out of there. I want to see this again."

When it was open, the hinged hatch did not rest on its back on the deck. It was held at a forty-five degree angle by a retaining chain. A few minutes later, the ship took another extra big roll, and the hatch was thrown back over and slammed shut with a bang again.

"I'll be damned," said Robado. "It's a disaster waiting to happen, and it did. Who would have rigged this thing that way? It should be down flat on the deck when it's open, or it should have a safety chain on the back side to keep it from closing. God, I may lose my job yet."

"Cap, open it up again." He did so. Joan continued, "What part of it hit him? Where would his head have been?"

He said, "He was lying that way, so it would be over here near the edge."

Joan looked closely at that area of the underside of the hatch. "Yep. Look right here," she said. "There's a bit of hair stuck in the wood grain. Ron has short light brown hair; this is his. Cap, you've got to get that tested for Ron's DNA. And the notebooks probably have Ron's prints on them."

"Yes indeed. Well, those fancy forensic boys sure never thought of that hatch cover as a potential weapon. Hundred bucks the prosecutor will still say Paul snuck up and slammed it on Withers. But I'm with you. Accident is the most likely thing here."

Joan nodded and said, "Set it up one more time. I want to get a video clip of this."

He opened the hatch again, and she captured the self-closing hatch process on her smartphone camera. "Got it."

"Okay," said Robado. "Let me close and lock this bastard, and give me those books. I'll go up and get on the horn to Traverse City."

Joan reached back in the hold and retrieved the backpack, put the notebooks in it, and gave it to the captain.

After calming down for a few minutes, Joan brought the messenger weight up on deck to the benthos crew. They had winched the Smith-McIntyre a few feet up off the bottom so that it would drift on the cable along with the ship as the wind pushed her sideways. They were still close enough to the plotted station location, so they lowered the sampler back onto the bottom and sent down the messenger. They were back in action. They finished the station, and *Halcyon* got underway eastward.

Captain Robado had taken the backpack containing the notebooks up to his cabin and put it next to his briefcase. For the call to Traverse City, *Halcyon* was less than halfway back across the lake from Wisconsin, and totally out of VHF range. Calling by radio through the marine operator in Racine was too much trouble, and Robado simply took the new satellite phone out on the bridge wing and dialed RULI headquarters directly. Mate Irv Thompson had the bridge watch, and he could hear Cap's end of the conversation with the operations superintendent. He listened spellbound.

"Dave, Robado here. What? Yeah, we're on our last few stations. Listen, fasten your seatbelt. I've got something huge here. Joan Brockton and I were down in that aft hold to get something, and we discovered that the goddamn hatch cover slams itself shut in a seaway. If it's open against that cockamamie chain somebody rigged on it, the son of a bitch gets thrown back over by a good starboard roll. A thirty-pound hammer airborne at forty miles an hour. Boss, I think what we had last week was one bad-ass accident. We were rolling like stink coming around the point that morning. Ron was probably down there then. What? Yeah, I suppose Tyson could have snuck up and thrown it over on him. I don't think he did though. Maybe he's been a little grumpy lately, but if you ask me, he's a solid standup guy.

"Look Dave, you gotta get those forensic wizards lined up to come back and lift Ron Withers' DNA off that hatch. Some of his hair is still stuck on it. They also need to check two notebooks belonging to Paul Tyson for Ron's fingerprints. Joan found them in that hold when we were down there. Withers was probably either stashing them or retrieving them when he got brained. Anyway, our ETA for the dock is nineteen hundred. Okay. Thanks Dave."

Mate Thompson's mouth was still frozen in a big round O when Cap came back in from the bridge wing.

"How 'bout them apples?" Robado said.

Thompson whistled long, high and loud. "I'll be dipped in shit. Makes more sense now. More reason to think Tyson's not the bad guy here, eh?"

"I hope so, Irv. I hope so. I do like the guy."

"So do I, Cap."

Then Robado looked through the window down at the foredeck, and he noticed Joan trying to make a call on her cell phone. She looked at it, shook her head in frustration, and closed it. Cap knew as well as she did that she was way out of cell tower range out here. He also knew who she was trying to call. He took the satellite phone out of his pocket and started below. She was in the bow staring forward toward Michigan in tears, when Cap reached gently for her hand and put the satellite phone in it.

"Try this one. It's a satellite phone."

She turned to him and broke into a smile that would light up Times Square like New Year's Eve. "You've made my day Cap."

"Well you're about to make his day, that's for sure." Robado moved off so she could have the foredeck to herself.

Joan stared eastward waiting for Paul to pick up.

"Paul?"

Silence from Paul; then, "It's you."

"Yes."

"Joan, I'm such an a..."

"Don't talk. You have to listen first. I'm still at sea. Paul, that hatch slams shut all by itself when we roll hard. It hit Ron while he was in there. They will find his DNA on it. It was an accident."

"Wait, wait, wait. Slow down. What hatch? What are you talking about?"

"I was down in that hold getting a messenger weight. The hatch cover nearly hit me while I was stooping down in the hold. Captain Robado and I watched it happen two more times, got it on video. Hair like Ron's is stuck to the underside of the hatch right above where Ron would have been according to his position when they found him. That's not all, Paul. I found your data books down in there in a backpack. They're going to look for his fingerprints on them."

Paul was speechless. *The backpack Withers was carrying....*

"Paul, I..."

"They're still going to think I did it. Slammed it on him."

"Paul, I don't want to talk about what they think right now. I know what *I* think. It's what I should have known all along."

"You didn't get much help from me."

"I shouldn't have needed any help from you. That's been your whole point, hasn't it, Paul?"

"I don't know that I could have put it into words, but now that you have, I guess that pretty much gets to the heart of it."

"Why couldn't I have understood that? Why was I being such an idiot?"

"Why was *I* being such an asshole?" replied Paul.

"Look, we're almost finished sampling and will be heading home. We should be docking around seven. Can you be there? We can talk all night then."

"Craig's got me quarantined here on my boat, but I'm going to violate that. I'll be there."

"What do you mean quarantined?"

"Not important now. I'll explain later. Make that damn boat go fast, Joan."

"I'm on my way to the engine room with a whip and a gun. Bye Paul."

# Chapter

## 18

After Joan's call, Paul immediately called Craig Basham and told him her news. "They're still going to prosecute me for hitting him with that hatch cover, Craig. My prints will be on it, just like everyone else's at RULI who has been in and out of that hold."

"Probably so," Craig replied. "And this won't help: I deposed Dr. Bates on Wednesday, and he still claims no knowledge of where you were. But there's something fishy about the way he answers questions, and I think he's lying or sitting on something. I don't have any way to get at it at this point. At least he's not saying he saw you below with Withers. Anyway, I'd say the popular sentiment will favor the accident theory now, since we now know it easily could have happened that way."

"You're kidding. You know better than I do that popular sentiment and a buck-fifty will get you a cardboard cup of lousy coffee in the courthouse. Craig, I'm coming in to meet Joan at the boat."

"I still don't want you in the same town with Larry Griffin, Paul."

"Griffin doesn't matter anymore."

"Okay, I'll buy that. It's good to hear that you and Joan have quit talking past each other."

"Got that right. Look, I need to call Dr. Perry and bring him up to date."

"Have a good weekend, partner, and hi to Joan."

Paul made the call to Perry and described Joan's discovery.

"Paul, I can't tell you how glad I am to hear this."

"I'm not out of the woods yet. Prosecutor's not going to let up. Especially now that those books make the motive appear even stronger."

"Lord, I guess you're right. But I never had a doubt, Paul. Not for one second."

"I don't know if I deserve that trust, the way I've acted through all this, starting with my high school locker room stunt in that cafeteria. Anyway, I want to meet Joan when *Halcyon* gets in this evening, so I'm going to come in this afternoon and reacquaint myself with the lab. Craig has released me from my quarantine up here."

"I don't know what that's about."

"You don't want to know, and it's history. I'll see you in a bit."

"Yep. Bye."

Paul closed his phone. He had taken Joan's call down in *Tondeleyo's* cabin, and he had stayed down there while making his two calls. Now he stepped up into the cockpit, into the brilliance of the Elk Rapids harbor. It was as though he could see color for the first time. He could smell the pungent harbor water. He could feel the sun-warmed teak under his hand. He could hear halyards slap and seagulls squeal.

He walked up to River Street actually feeling hungry, and the sandwich did not taste like sawdust as it had for two weeks. Walking back down to the harbor Paul was reminded of the way he had always felt as a boy walking home from school on the first day of summer vacation.

Paul took his Mustang through its gears and out of Elk Rapids, south toward Traverse City. His mind was ticking over as fast as the engine was along the fifteen mile drive to the institute, and he arrived in the parking lot with a plan that he had to run by Dr. Perry. On the way into the building, a couple of people gave him big grins as he passed by. *News travels fast. Let's not count our chickens now, folks.*

Perry welcomed Paul into his office with a vigorous handshake. "Good to see you Paul."

"Likewise, Dr. Perry. Listen, I need to run something up the flag pole. Maybe it seems out of place to worry about this right now, but I'm getting totally stalled out here in my research. Most importantly, as things stand I'm going to miss my scheduled phytoplankton survey in my study area. I'm not allowed on the *Halcyon* or the *Chinook*. Ron Withers has obviously settled into a very long coma, and the case seems to be going at a snail's pace. Is there any possibility I could go out and do my sampling transects in my own boat? It would take about a week, and I could stay in touch and return early if necessary."

Dr. Perry leaned back and stroked his jaw. "I like the idea, but I doubt if the prosecutor will. What I'll need to do first is to get Karen Tollefson in our camp. What may help are those new satellite phones we have that transmit the GPS location of the phone. You could check in with one of those as often as they want you to. And you're not exactly going to outrun anyone in a six-knot displacement hull. I'll call and see if Tollefson will see me right now. I haven't even had a chance to tell her about Joan's news."

Paul went to the lab. Perry called upstairs and then went up to the director's suite.

"Karen, I have some good news and a proposition."

"I think I know your good news; Dave called me late this morning about the hatch. But a proposition? Jim, you're a swell guy, but I've been married for twenty years."

Perry grinned, and launched into an explanation of Paul's idea. When he finished, Tollefson gave it some thought.

"Jim, we've been behind Paul pretty much all along in this, and the news that an accident can explain the whole thing is very welcome indeed. I think we should help him all we can. Now I have a strong hunch that the prosecutor would nix this idea in a heartbeat. But with the satellite phone in on it, I guess I'm willing to go all the way out on the limb and interpret it as just an extension of his work here at RULI. By that I mean, don't ask, don't tell. But I want Paul to come up here so I can talk to him about it myself."

Five minutes later Paul was sitting in the director's office. Dr. Tollefson looked straight at Paul over her reading glasses. "Paul, against my better judgment I'm going to allow you to do your survey on your boat. I'm stretching my neck all the way out on a chopping block right in front of the prosecutor, and handing him the axe. But the way things are, my job is in jeopardy anyway, along with Dave Washington's and Tony Robado's. Even if you are eventually cleared, a Withers family lawsuit could shake RULI to its foundations. Anyway, you are to file a detailed float plan with Dave Washington, and you are to call him every four hours on the satellite phone to confirm your location. Day and night. Set an alarm at night. The night watchman will answer and record your calls. Cross me up on this, Paul, and I'll be tempted to sink that boat of yours. I'll have nothing to lose by then."

Paul was stunned. He had figured that this attractive, accomplished scientist was probably something of a scrapper to get where she was in her career. She had just removed all doubt.

"Dr. Tollefson, to be honest, I hardly expected this idea to fly. You are more than generous to take this chance on me. You won't be disappointed."

"Okay Paul. Get on with it. This stack of paper here isn't going anywhere by itself."

Paul went down to Dr. Perry's office. He gave Perry the thumbs up sign at the doorway, and Perry returned the sign with a grin. Paul went on down the hall to the lab and got out his list of equipment and supplies for his Lake Michigan sampling regime. It was a long list and he started getting the stuff organized. There was one thing missing on the list, however. A technical assistant. Paul didn't normally have to be concerned about that, as there were always a number of student hands on the *Halcyon* cruises. No such thing on his own boat. His eyes narrowed as he looked at his watch, and he gazed out the window at the harbor. It would be a long afternoon waiting for Joan to get back. He got busy again with the sampling equipment.

# Chapter
# *19*

After Joan called Paul from the *Halcyon*, she went up to the bridge to thank the captain again. He nodded, and then asked her to email the video clip to him when they got back into cell tower range. Joan went back down on deck and participated in the remaining two sampling stations, and then she settled down to wait out the slow ride to home port. Twelve knots seemed like two.

At seven forty-five p.m., the RULI harbor was finally in view. So was Paul. He was sitting on the same bollard she was on while waiting for him two weeks ago. *Halcyon* slowly came alongside, and Paul took the hawsers from the deck hands. Captain Robado watched from the bridge as Paul then took Joan's sea bag from her, and they walked directly toward his car. In full view of half the ship's company, they did not pause for any dramatic embracing.

They put Joan's bag in the backseat and climbed in, and the Mustang headed around the foot of the bay for Elk Rapids at a leisurely pace of about forty-five. The sun was still well above the horizon, but a riotous contest between reds and pinks began to unfold all over the western sky.

Joan spoke first. "The Larry Griffin thing, Paul, I…"

"You don't need to explain anything, Joan."

"Yes, I do. Please let me get it out."

Paul was silent.

"Last Friday afternoon I just wanted to go have a damn beer. I was getting to be crazier than a rat in a tin shithouse,

Paul. I was screwing up in the lab like a freshman in Chem 101 with two left hands. The fucking hazmat people had to come in there. Then Larry appeared at the lab out of nowhere, and I jumped at the invitation like a wide-eyed frat-party girl. One beer turned into a bunch of them, and I caved in to a dinner date for Saturday, for Christ sake. The bastard got me drunk again, and we somehow wound up at my place."

Paul's grip tightened on the wheel.

"Then he told me about Bates being in his cabin all that morning. Larry was trying to talk his way into my pants. It wasn't working, so he tried threatening to testify against you. I threw him out. There was never a chance in hell, Paul."

Paul relaxed his grip a little. "I have no doubt about that, Joan." But he did not say how he'd felt all week until her call this morning.

"It was the worst day of my entire life," Joan continued. "But it's over. I don't want you to even think about confronting him."

"No need to. If that's the way he works, he'll most likely get himself thrown out of the university on a sexual harassment charge by some young coed, or several, before the year is out."

They were quiet for a while, and then Paul told Joan about his plan to get his sampling done.

"Can you get away for another week? I need an assistant and a deck hand. You can be both. In fact I won't go, if you can't do it."

"When do we leave?"

"Tomorrow we can provision and load up equipment, and get underway on Sunday morning."

"I'm in, Paul."

They pulled into the Elk Rapids harbor lot, and went down to Paul's boat. Standing in the cockpit in the incandescent sunset, they locked in a long embrace that could have squeezed water out of a stone.

Saturday morning they drove back to Traverse City. From the institute lot, Joan drove her Blazer to her apartment to wash clothes and repack her sea bag. Paul went into the lab and gathered all the sampling gear: a Van Dorn water sampler, plastic sample bottles, marking pens, iodine preservative, multi-parameter underwater sensing probe, notebook, and chart of his sampling stations. He checked the batteries in the probe and its readout module and calibrated all of the sensor functions. He carried the four plastic crates of this equipment out to the trunk of his car and went back in and got one of the satellite phones from David Washington in the headquarters office. He gave Washington his float plan, and they set up a call schedule.

"You say Tollefson wants the calls every four hours around the clock?" asked Washington.

"Yes," replied Paul.

"Then let's have you call at eight, twelve and four, both a.m. and p.m. That way I can take the three daytime calls, and the night security man can take the three overnight calls. And you'll probably only need to set an alarm for the oh-four-hundred call."

"Lovely," said Paul.

"Hey, not my idea, my friend."

"I know. Lucky I can do this, so no complaints, really. Otherwise, there would be a big hole in my data set. I can just see the graphs. A blank space with an asterisk."

"What would the asterisk's footnote say?"

"Data not available – author incarcerated."

"Paul, I'm real sorry you're going through this."

"Thanks Dave. I'll be talking to you."

Paul went out to his car. He picked up Joan at her place, and they drove back up to Elk Rapids. At the grocery on Ames Street they loaded up with a week's worth of food and beer and spent a leisurely afternoon on *Tondeleyo* getting everything stowed and secured for the cruise. Paul checked the crankcase oil and ran the engine for a while to make sure there were no surprises there. He made sure all of his electronics were working, as well as the running lights. Finally he hosed down the deck and filled the freshwater tank. He would top off the fuel tank and pump out the head's holding tank on the way out in the morning.

Paul then called Craig Basham and told him where he would be for the next week and that he would be communicating with Dave Washington at RULI by satellite phone.

"Okay," Craig said. "I will be working on convincing the prosecutor to drop the charges. Going to remind him that Occam's razor now overwhelmingly favors the accident theory."

"Who's what? Oh, of course. 'The simplest explanation for something is most probably the correct one.'"

"Applies in law just like it does in science, dude."

"Prosecutor buys that, I'll start munching on my favorite hat."

"Unfortunately, Paul, your hat's pretty safe. These pit bull prosecutors, it takes a very big crow bar to pry their jaws off their own theories. We're working with a toothpick here. Gotta keep prying though. Listen, are you sure you want your notebooks dusted for Withers' prints? They'll just apply toward motive."

"Yes I do. I want the truth known."

"Ron Withers is already paying a pretty steep price for his actions, Paul."

"Look, it may be hard to believe, but in spite of my stupid loss of control in that cafeteria, I was never really after Ron to be injured, or even punished in some other way. I just want Dr. Perry and me to have *our* scientific integrity protected. When I presented my data in Ann Arbor, someone recognized our data from reading Ron's paper and seemed to be asking where *we* got the data. That got the audience's full attention, believe me. And until the truth of Ron's theft comes out, and they publish a retraction, we can't publish my data. That's three years of work down the drain. Not to mention the tens of thousands of dollars of grant money supporting it. Do you get the picture Craig?"

"Loud and clear. Paul, have a good trip. I will call you if anything new comes up."

With everything squared away on *Tondeleyo*, Paul and Joan went to dinner over on Ames Street. Paul wasn't that much of a Cajun food fan, but he knew that Joan loved it.

"I hadn't looked at it quite that way either, Paul," said Joan over coffee.

"What are you talking about?"

"Your phone conversation with Craig back on the boat. The importance of getting credit for your own data."

"I wasn't seeing things too clearly either in Ann Arbor."

"Let's hope Craig can get that prosecutor seeing straight."

They paid the bill and decided to try another movie on River Street. This time they did enjoy the film, even though it was a largely forgettable potboiler. Later, after a walk up the street and back, they settled in *Tondeleyo's* cockpit with a couple of Coronas.

Gazing around at the tranquil harbor, Joan asked, "Has this place always been this way?"

"No," replied Paul. "According to documents up there in the town historical museum, the legend is that the first European-American to visit the site saw a large elk rack lying on the banks of the river that flowed into the bay, and named it the Elk River. As there were rapids there, the village that sprang up naturally became Elk Rapids, and the inland lake flowing into the river became Elk Lake, the final jewel in the chain of lakes that includes the more famous Torch Lake.

"Very soon the chain of lakes became a conduit for the water transport of the millions of logs cut throughout this region in the logging boom of the eighteen hundreds, and Elk

Rapids was one of the major ports of export for this trade. A moderate sized iron works was also built in Elk Rapids, as was that power dam over there to capitalize on the strong river flow. Elk Rapids bustled with all of this commerce for several decades, and this harbor was all business and probably not very clean."

"Then what happened?" asked Joan.

"Well, the town fell into relative insignificance in the early and mid twentieth century, as logging here faded into history and larger steel companies became dominant elsewhere. Meanwhile, the tourist industry began reshaping the major destinations of Charlevoix, Petoskey, Harbor Springs and Mackinac Island, but Elk Rapids was slow to catch on and remained a backwater for years. But more recently tourism seems to have provided funds enough to spruce up the place nicely. Many of the original buildings still stand, and special among those is the village library right above us there. But it wasn't a library for quite a while. It was built in 1865 as the private residence house of businessman E. S. Noble, who called it 'Island House.'

"Anyway, I sort of fell in love with this place the first time I saw it, and I came here often. Prowling the docks led me to my friendship with Ian Kerrigan. On *Tondeleyo* we cruised to many fine harbors on Lake Michigan and Lake Huron, but Elk Rapids has remained my favorite."

Paul and Joan fell silent, and watched the many people strolling the docks in the pleasant Saturday evening breeze. A hundred or so service pedestal lamps glowed all around the marina and reflected off the glassy water. A piano sonata tinkled softly somewhere from the cockpit speakers of one of the other boats, nearly lost in the muffled hiss of water over at the power dam outflow. A young girl giggled near the gazebo, and a loon flying over from the Elk River marshes echoed with its own long burst of hilarity. A seagull peeled out a final chorus of bleating calls.

Paul pulled the satellite phone and his own cell phone from his pockets and switched them off. Joan did the same with her phone, and they went below.

# Chapter
## *20*

Sunday, June 27, Paul and Joan rose to a fine morning with high, light cirrus clouds riding the ten knot wind diagonally across the bay toward the northeast. The southwest wind was perfect for the course they would be sailing. Dressed in deck shoes, cargo pants, windbreakers, and wind keepers clipped in back of their ball caps, they walked up to a coffee house on River Street and bought a table full of hot cereal, scrambled eggs, Canadian bacon, OJ and coffee. They lingered a little while over a second cup, got a thermos bottle filled with the excellent brew and headed back to the boat.

Paul unhooked the two yellow shore power cables from the service pedestal and stowed them in their seat locker. While the engine was warming up at idle, Paul and Joan unfastened the StackPack sail covers on the main and mizzen sails. Everything was ready. At Paul's nod, Joan lifted the lines off the dock cleats and brought them aboard, and Paul gave the boat a short burst of reverse.

A family of four was watching them from the sea wall, and the young dad came out on the finger dock wanting to lend a hand.

"Yeah, you can give the bow pulpit a shove out to our right when it clears the dock piling. Thanks," said Paul.

The guy watched as Paul shifted into forward to start *Tondeleyo* moving out toward the fuel dock. On the sea wall, the man's wife sniped, "Quit dreaming Brent. We can't afford a rowboat." Brent turned back up the finger dock.

"Hang in there pal," offered Paul.

With a full tank of diesel and an empty holding tank, Paul nosed *Tondeleyo* away from the fuel dock and took her out through the breakwater channel. He took it slow, with one eye on the depth gage. Sand constantly accumulated here, and *Tondeleyo's* five and a half foot draft was on his mind. Once before he had plowed a little of it with his keel – no problem, but he didn't ever want to get brought up hard. Clearing the channel, Paul turned to port, due west. Paul's first sampling station was right off Elk Rapids in the middle of the East Arm of the bay, so they didn't bother to raise sail yet. The station's coordinates were in the waypoint log of *Tondeleyo's* GPS, and the instrument beeped to signal that they were approaching the location.

As *Tondeleyo* arrived on station, Paul turned left ten degrees to put the bow into the wind, and shifted to neutral. Leaving the engine running at idle, he asked Joan to stand by at the wheel and watch the GPS, and give *Tondeleyo* a brief nudge forward into the wind now and then to keep her on station.

Turning to his equipment, Paul first assembled the multi parameter probe unit, connecting the sensor cable to the readout unit. He switched it on, set it in recording mode and entered the station number and date. From the deck beside the cockpit, he hung the sensor head into the surface water and waited a few minutes for it to equilibrate to the conditions in the water. Then he lowered it slowly meter by meter, watching the data on the screen of the readout unit. It was telling him the depth, temperature, pH, conductivity, bound carbon dioxide (as carbonate alkalinity), oxygen, turbidity, and algal chlorophyll biomass.

Paul did not have to write any of the data down, as it was being recorded in the unit's memory, but he paid particular attention to the temperature. He wanted to know the depth at which there was a rapid transition from relatively warm water to much colder water, known as the thermocline.

For his phytoplankton work, he was interested only in the warmer upper layer known as the epilimnion, because that was where the living, growing algae were. Below that, there was not enough light for photosynthesis. When the sensor reached the thermocline, Paul pulled it back up to the surface. He attached a data cable to his laptop computer and downloaded the data as a backup to the data in the probe's memory. He then switched off the probe and stowed it.

Joan shifted *Tondeleyo* into forward and headed her up into the wind for a couple of minutes, then back into neutral.

Paul cocked open the large rubber stoppers at each end of the cylindrical Van Dorn water sampler, and held it by its cable just under the water surface. He dropped the messenger weight to trip the sampler closed and returned the unit on deck. From the spigot he filled a plastic sample bottle. He repeated this twice more to obtain triplicate surface samples. Then he lowered the sampler halfway down in the epilimnion three times to get triplicate samples from there.

"It sure is a pain to have to take these samples one at a time," said Paul.

"You need to install a big winch and a davit," Joan replied. She was referring to the oceanographic-style rig on the *Halcyon* that allowed deployment of multiple water sampler clusters arrayed on a cable at all of the depth positions simultaneously. Only one cast was needed to obtain all of the samples at a given station.

"Yeah, we're kind of doing rowboat limnology here," said Paul.

As Paul filled a plastic sample bottle, Joan asked, "So how do you concentrate the algae to identify and count them? I mean, why aren't you using a plankton net?"

"Phytoplankton people haven't used nets for years. Turns out that the majority of species are too small to be captured by nets of any mesh size that they make, and a smaller mesh size would clog up fast and be useless. They're called nanoplankton and picoplankton."

"Yeah, I've heard of them. So what do you do with the water samples?"

"After preserving them with Lugol's, a special iodine solution, back in the lab we put a known volume in the vertical cylinder of a settling chamber apparatus, and let the algal cells and colonies sink down overnight onto a glass slide in the base. Remove the slide, add a permanent cover slip, and you have all of the algae from that sample volume visible in an inverted phase-contrast microscope.

"We have two six-place units, so we can settle a dozen samples at once. The slides can accumulate and be analyzed any time in the future. Keeps those long winter days full of excitement."

"Like the excitement of waiting for an electrophoresis run in my DNA work," Joan replied dryly.

"Yeah well, all lab work is tedious, isn't it." agreed Paul. "The excitement is in asking the questions, designing the experiments, and most of all seeing the answers being revealed as the data unfold."

"No doubt about that. But those of us who also go into the field sure get a bonus. Don't tell the pure lab pukes that."

"They know," said Paul, "and they think we're just skylarking out here."

"Let them try it when it's cold, raining, and blowing so bad it's like you're trying to get an accurate sample on the back of a rodeo bull."

For his third and final set of samples here at Station 1, Paul lowered the sampler to the thermocline at the bottom of the epilimnion. He sent the messenger down.

"That didn't feel right," Paul said, pulling the sampler back toward the surface.

"What do you mean?" asked Joan.

"Don't think it tripped. Yep, look at the bastard. Have to re-cock and go back down. Hangs up pretty often. Too goddamn often. I'd like to SHOOT the guy that designed it"

"Listen to yourself, Paul."

"Still shooting my mouth off, right?" said Paul as he reset the sampler. "Well, I'm pretty sure old Professor Van Dorn has long since gone to his reward; if not, he'd be pretty safe from me over in Europe somewhere."

"Your bark is worse than your bite, Captain Tyson, even if you do kind of look like a tough guy."

"Craig might have to call you as a witness. 'His bark is worse than his bite, your honor.' That should do the trick."

"They'll think I was paid to give such high praise. But Paul, this isn't so damn funny."

"No shit."

Paul lowered the sampler. It worked this time, and it worked for the second and third replicates as well. Paul added the preservative to all of the bottles, and stowed the sample box and the Van Dorn.

Before leaving Station 1, Paul called the institute on the satellite phone. It was closer to nine a.m. than to eight, but this was Paul's first stop, and they were still essentially in Elk Rapids. David Washington noted that the GPS readout from the sat phone matched the coordinates of Station 1 in Paul's float plan and recorded that fact along with the time of the call in the "Paul Tyson Log" he would keep during Paul's trip. Paul said that he would call again at Station 2, which was about four hours north.

To get back underway, Paul had Joan head into the wind at slow forward. Paul first raised the mizzen sail aft, which would act as a weather vane to help keep *Tondeleyo* headed into the wind. Then up went the main sail, winch handle clanking into its socket and then winch gears clicking steadily as the Dacron rose, blinding white in the sun. The luffing main and mizzen roared and rattled with the staccato sound of a pair of fifty-caliber machine guns while Paul drew out the roller furled Genoa jib to its full 120 percent dimension.

"Let her fall off gradually, and steer due north," Paul shouted over the booming racket of the now three luffing sails. As Joan steadied on course, Paul adjusted the sheets of all three sails so that they filled perfectly in the broad reach that already had them creaming along at nearly five knots. Paul returned the engine to neutral, shut it off, and punched Go To Station 2 into the GPS. He let Joan continue to steer, guided now by the GPS track indicator instead of the compass, and went below to pour them both some coffee from the thermos.

Holding the steaming mugs in the cockpit, they sat in silence while the cool stiff breeze buffeted their faces and the sun-sparkled bay dazzled their eyes. Two miles away on each side of them, pale yellow sand beaches stretched along in front of evergreen and birch woods on low hills; ahead of them was a landless horizon of blue on blue. The only sound was the bow wave unfolding into a white-noise hiss along the hull. Altogether it was an unspeakable high, like a mainlined drug without which every veteran sailor goes into withdrawal when out of reach of navigable water.

"Paul, this is just unbelievable," said Joan, her cap off and hair blowing in the wind. "What could be better?"

"Well, the Grenadine Islands in the southern Caribbean are supposed to be about the best cruising grounds anywhere. I sailed them with Ian Kerrigan on a bareboat charter a few winters ago, and they are truly amazing, especially the Tobago Cays. But, except for the lack of marine reef snorkeling and diving here, to me the beauty of the sailing experience in the bays, islands, and open water of the northern Great Lakes comes pretty damn close."

They continued to enjoy the ride in silence. After an hour at the wheel, Joan turned it over to Paul and went below to build some heroic ham and cheese sandwiches for lunch. She came back up with a couple of apples for the rest of

Paul's hour on watch. Just before noon, Joan ate her sandwich and then took the wheel for her watch, and Paul tucked into his sandwich. The rest of the thermos coffee washed down the sandwiches, and they settled down for the final miles to Station 2.

Paul made his noon call to Dave Washington. "Hey Dave. We're approaching Station 2. It will be too late to make both Stations 3 and 4 today, and 3 is not near enough to a good port for the night, so we are heading for Charlevoix. We'll hit 3 and 4 tomorrow. Thanks Dave."

At shortly after one pm, *Tondeleyo* arrived at Station 2 at the head of Grand Traverse Bay, half way between the tip of the Leelanau peninsula and the village of Norwood on the Michigan mainland. With her engine running and Joan holding her into the wind, Paul furled the jenny and then lowered the main and mizzen into their StackPacks on the booms. He got out all the sampling equipment and repeated the routine that he had gone through at Station 1. A multi parameter probe profile and three replicate water samples each at the surface, halfway down the epilimnion and at the thermocline. The Van Dorn hung up twice at this station, accompanied by more barrages of cursing, but by one forty-five p.m. they were finished.

Before getting underway, Paul dialed the number of the owner of a small boatyard in Charlevoix. "Mr. McAllister, this is Paul Tyson. Don't know if you remember me, but I was crewing for Ian Kerrigan when we berthed many times at your yard. You do? Great. Yeah, he died a couple of years ago; I have the boat now. Listen, do you have dock space for me this evening? That would be great. I love your yard, and I hate the prices on the city waterfront. Okay, we will be there in few hours. Thanks a bunch Mr. McAllister. Okay, Marty it is. It'll be good to see you too. Bye now."

"Okay, we're all set for a nice quiet place to dock overnight that won't cost an arm and a leg," Paul said to Joan. "The owner and Ian were real buddies."

Again Joan motored *Tondeleyo* slowly upwind while Paul raised sail. The wind had picked up to fifteen knots, and they would be sailing almost directly downwind on their northeasterly course to Charlevoix, so Paul left the main sail down. It wouldn't be needed, and the danger of an accidental jibe of that big sail was too great. Up went the mizzen and out came the jib. After Joan let *Tondeleyo* fall around to their course, Paul shut off the engine. Then he rigged a jibe preventer for the mizzen, running a line from a bale on the boom forward to a snatch block on the rail and back to a quick-release jam cleat near the cockpit coaming.

They were set for the downwind sleigh ride. The following waves rose under *Tondeleyo's* stern and lifted her majestically, and as each wave passed forward, her big cruising hull bowed into the trough like a grand dame making a curtsey to the queen. White spray flared to the sides like glimpses of petticoats. Wheeling and crying gulls were following them now, adding their cheer to the glorious run to Charlevoix.

Also tagging along was the shadow of Paul's albatross, keeping pace with the boat, its wing-beats relentlessly whispering, *Withers, Withers, Withers....* It had been there all day, as though tethered to the boat on a kite string. But the sailing remained superb, and it was impossible not to enjoy it. Even with the distraction of making the four p.m. call to the institute.

# CHAPTER 21

Having reached the Charlevoix breakwater, Paul sailed *Tondeleyo* back and forth outside the channel for twenty minutes waiting for the six p.m. opening of the drawbridge. Then he rounded up, dropped the mizzen, furled the jenny and motored into the channel along with two other sailboats that had been waiting. The three-boat parade slowly slid by the restaurants and condos lining the channel in the lowering afternoon sun, blissfully blocking traffic on Bridge Street which was the U.S. 31 thoroughfare through town.

Passing the bridge and entering Round Lake, Paul called Martin McAllister and informed him they would be arriving at his boatyard in a few minutes. *Tondeleyo* passed by the lineup of gold platers in the expensive slips along the city seawall and approached the southern shore of the small circular lake that served as a fully protected natural yacht basin. This appropriately named lake also served as the conduit for water flowing from Lake Charlevoix out into Lake Michigan.

McAllister's was a small family owned boatyard that was a throwback to the days before the modern mega-marinas. Martin, a ruddy faced caricature of an old sea dog in a Greek fisherman's cap and navy blue turtleneck, was out at the end of one of his two docks. He motioned with a gnarled hand for Paul to pull in right where he was standing.

Paul laid the starboard side along the dock, and Joan handed Martin a line as Paul stopped *Tondeleyo* with several seconds of reverse thrust. Paul stepped onto the dock with another line, but before he could get it onto a piling, McAllister attacked him with a bear hug and a roaring welcome.

"Guud to see ya, me booy. Now, what kennah do furr ya?"

Paul staggered back from the bear hug. "You look like you can still carry one end of a sixty-foot pine mast, Marty. Get me a couple cases of whatever you're drinking these days! But really, just let me hook up to your shore power and tell me what I owe you for the night."

"Sockets are roight there by yer bow, an' ya don't owe me a penny."

"Oh come on Marty."

"Nay, nay. Any man that ol' Ian truusted enuuf ta have as parmanent crew, and luuved enough ta give his booat when he left this world, that man is me guest. *Tondeleyo* belongs here, son. I only ask ya tell all yer friends McAllister's Booatyaard's the best place ta fix an' store yer booat."

"Well I'll sure do that." Paul replied. "Looks like I'm lucky there was one spot left open here."

"There warn't, till ah pulled me work booat up on the rails ashore there."

"Marty, this is too much. But I'm grateful," Paul said. Then he finally noticed Joan still standing on the deck, and he slapped himself on the forehead. "Holy mackerel, I'm forgetting my damn manners. Marty, meet my special friend here, Joan Brockton. She's a fellow grad student down at the institute in Traverse."

"What manners?" Joan joked, and then extended her hand. "Mr. McAllister, it's a pleasure."

"Not half so muuch as mine, sweethaart, not half so muuch. Yer a soite furr these ol' eyes, that's furr shurre. Well, you yuungsters get yer booat tied up proper then. I'll be uup at the hoouse, ya need ennathing."

"Thanks again, Marty," Paul called out as McAllister walked back up the dock toward his work shed, his bow legs churning and elbows pumping.

Paul and Joan hung a couple of fenders and finished tying up the boat. Paul hooked up the thirty-amp shore cable but didn't bother with the fifty-amp one, as that was for the air conditioner/heater circuit that he wouldn't need tonight. Just as well, he realized. Marty didn't have any fifty-amp outlets.

Joan went below, opened a can of beef stew and heated up two big bowls of it in the microwave. She threw together a simple salad, and rounded out the meal with some bread and butter and two dripping cold cans of Miller Highlife.

Paul slid in opposite Joan at the teak settee. There was teak and mahogany all over the roomy salon, and it glowed like gold in the soft lighting from the early evening sun streaming through the starboard portholes. They clinked their beer cans together in a silent toast, and hungrily tucked into the meal. The pilings and fenders creaked as *Tondeleyo* gently worked at her dock lines in the falling breeze.

"Marty is some character," said Joan.

"And how," replied Paul.

"He must have had quite an attachment to Kerrigan and this boat."

"They were inseparable buddies from way back."

"Where did the name *Tondeleyo* come from?" asked Joan.

"Ian said something about a novel he read long ago with a heroine who was a magnificent African queen of that name. He fell in love with the sound of it. Later, when he built this boat, he painted the hull black and put her name on the transom."

"Nice story," replied Joan. "That reminds me. The name *Halcyon*. Isn't that some drug?"

"No, it just means peaceful. You know, 'the halcyon days of yore' and all that? The sedative by that name is spelled with an 'i' instead of the 'y', but they're obviously alluding to the pleasant notion of the original word."

"Some peaceful ship!" said Joan.

"Right."

After they cleaned up the dinnerware, Paul made his scheduled call to Dave Washington at headquarters, which was getting tiresome. They showered and changed into clean jeans and shirts, and got ready for a walk over to the center of things on Bridge Street. They locked up *Tondeleyo* and walked off the dock and up the hill through the boatyard full of old wooden boats sagging on blocks and jack stands, including full keel sailing scows and vintage Chris-Crafts.

Reaching the tree-lined sidewalk on Belvedere Avenue, they walked westward past cottages, old book stores and antique shops toward Bridge Street. In the daylight savings time of northwestern Michigan in late June, darkness would not arrive until around ten pm.

Turning north on Bridge Street, they became entrained in the growing stream of locals, summer residents, and tourists out to enjoy the Charlevoix waterfront and its array of boutiques and bars. The numerous houses and small buildings with cedar shake siding made Charlevoix even more reminiscent of Martha's Vineyard than was Elk Rapids. The lineup of large yachts along the seawall on Round Lake was astonishing; but even though *Tondeleyo* would not have been out of place here, Paul much preferred the quaint seclusion of McAllister's yard.

"This is quite a scene," said Joan.

"Yeah, it's fun to come here now and then. But I still like Elk Rapids better. Smaller, quieter. Just as pretty."

They wandered along for a bit before ducking into one of the pubs, where they enjoyed the convivial crowd and some good draft beer for a while. At nine-thirty they called it a night and headed back to the boat in the twilight.

Paul had to kill some time before his midnight call-in. Joan played rummy with him for awhile, but eventually begged off to hit the sack. Paul got out one of his "boat books" (the paperbacks boaters swap with each other whenever they can) and gamely tried to follow the plot, but he kept nodding off. He needed an alarm, but he didn't want it to wake Joan, so he went up on deck where it was chilly now. He stared at the lights of Charlevoix across the harbor.

Lost in thought, Paul alternated between agonizing over the Withers mess and feeling damn lucky to have Joan here helping with his sampling run. He looked down into the salon below and saw her slumbering in the soft glow of the single cabin light that was still on. *That's an amazing woman down there.*

Finally midnight came, and Paul stepped onto the dock and moved out of earshot of the boat. He made his call to headquarters, which was answered and recorded again by the night watchman. Paul set his wristwatch alarm for four AM, hoping it wouldn't wake Joan then. This call schedule was going to be Chinese water torture. But Paul was not going to cross Director Tollefson. He stepped back aboard and went below to sleep.

# Chapter 22

Monday morning, Paul woke up only two hours after his four a.m. call-in. He could not get back to sleep, so he quietly got a cup of orange juice and went up on deck to let Joan sleep a while longer. The night's cold air lingered as the morning unfolded itself gently, not a ripple on the water except for the dripping from dew-laden docks and boat gunwales.

Gulls greeted the just-risen sun with bleating cries, anxious to get the day's foraging underway. Early morning in a harbor was a treasure for Paul. *Just need some coffee to make it perfect.* Paul could almost smell it. He did smell it. Joan appeared at the salon ladder with two steaming mugs of it.

"You're an angel of mercy," Paul said.

"Yeah? Well, my halo's a little rusty."

"A little Rustoleum from the paint locker will fix that," Paul replied. "Come on up and see this gorgeous morning."

Joan did that, and they took their time drinking the coffee.

"We might be motoring today if some wind doesn't come up," Paul said.

"And fighting the flies out there too." Joan replied. "Pray for wind."

Empty mugs prompted them to go below to get a breakfast going.

By seven-thirty the southwest wind had come back alive, and after clearing the breakwater they set all three sails and were close-hauled on a northwest course for Station 3. The sampling station was about fourteen miles offshore, nearly equidistant between Charlevoix and the southern end of Beaver Island. Gulls followed them all the way out, and at ten-thirty they were on station. Joan headed *Tondeleyo* up into the wind, and Paul dropped the sails. He made his eight a.m. call-in; Dave Washington was back in the office to take the call. Paul then got started with the sampling regime. Joan went below for a couple of bananas and fed one to Paul while he worked.

The station went smoothly, and they got underway for Station 4, about eighteen miles to the north-northeast. They were now back on a broad reach and sailing very well in a ten knot breeze. The day was clear again with only a few small cirrus clouds high in the northern sky.

Around noon, Paul called in while Joan went below and made another lunch of huge sandwiches and a thermos of coffee. They ate in the cockpit while boiling along with the bright sun high in the sky behind them.

At two-thirty p.m. they arrived at Station 4 which lay approximately equidistant between Cross Village on the mainland and the northern end of Beaver Island. Paul and Joan performed the now-familiar sampling routine. Finishing at shortly after three p.m., they again had the problem that if they went on up to Station 5 today, it would get too late to make port comfortably that evening. So they got underway on a northwesterly course for St. James Harbor on Beaver Island, sailing close-hauled again in a rising breeze. Paul reported the plan to Dave Washington.

When they were within a few miles of the harbor, Paul called the marina on channel 16 and learned that they had a transient slip available. At shortly before six p.m. they passed the Whiskey Point Lighthouse marking the north side of the harbor, rounded into the wind and dropped sails. They motored over to the marina, a stone's throw from the dock that serves the Beaver Island ferry out of Charlevoix.

Paul and Joan tied up *Tondeleyo* in one of the large slips on the outer end of the dock, switched off the engine, fastened the StackPacks over the main and mizzen, and hooked up the shore power. They walked to the marina office where they registered and paid the night's dockage fee.

They were not overly tired from the day's work, and Joan suggested they go for a run before dinner. Paul wasn't so sure, but agreed anyway. He suggested they head around on Michigan Avenue to the lighthouse and back. That would total a couple of miles. They returned to the boat and got into shorts and sneakers.

Joan was the runner, and she set a brisk pace. As a high school defensive back, Paul had been more of a short distance sprinter, and he hadn't done any running lately. A half mile into the run, he was laboring pretty hard, but was damned if he was going to complain. Joan was just getting warmed up and breathing easy.

They chugged on, and by the time they reached Whiskey Point light, Paul was twenty yards behind Joan and gasping. She gave Paul a break and slowed to a walk and circled the light tower. She didn't say anything about Paul's lack of conditioning; it was obvious.

They tried to enter the light tower to see the view, but they were disappointed to find it closed. They walked over to the beach and could see the marina back across the head of the bay that they had just circled. They decided to walk the beach northward around the point before jogging back. It was pleasantly out of sight of town, and shorebirds and gulls were everywhere. To the north they could see Garden Island just across the channel, and Hog Island was low in the hazy distance to the northeast.

"Station Five is several miles the other side of Hog Island over there," Paul said.

"This is an amazing sight," Joan replied. "Like pictures I've seen of the Caribbean, without the palms trees, of course."

"That's right."

They continued a little to the west on the beach and then turned south across the narrow neck of the point back to Michigan Avenue along the bay. Joan started running again, and Paul gamely got in gear too. He felt a lot better after the walking and kept up with Joan the rest of the mile back to the marina.

After hot showers at the marina office, they dressed in clean shorts, RULI sweatshirts and boat shoes, and walked the short distance over to Main Street to choose a restaurant. They found a nice one and went in to be seated. A couple of Coronas kept them company while they ordered some deluxe burgers and salads.

"I saw a sign for Kings Highway," said Paul as he squeezed his lime into the bottle. "What king do you suppose they're honoring?"

"That would be King James," Joan replied.

"The King James Bible guy?"

"No no. Don't you know the Beaver Island history?" said Joan. "Guy named James Strang set up a Mormon colony here back in the nineteenth century, the eighteen forties I think. He defied Brigham Young's authority, declared Beaver Island an independent kingdom and declared himself king. It was the only monarchy in U.S. history."

"I'll be damned. Christ, all I need now is for the cops to find out I've left the country."

"Don't tell anyone."

"Dave Washington already knows."

"Anyway, things didn't go so well for Strang; he was a bit of a tyrant, and he was shot dead by some of his subjects less than ten years into his reign. I don't think he's actually honored by much of anyone these days. But place names tend to stick around; ergo, Kings Highway."

"Did his majesty have a navy?"

"I don't think he had so much as a clue. But he did have a REAL BAD TEMPER, Mr. Tyson, and see where that got him?"

"Ouch."

Mercifully the burgers arrived, and the subject got dropped as they got busy eating.

On the way back to the marina they passed a bar with blacked-out windows and a handwritten sign on the door that proclaimed "TONIGHT ONLY – SIDEWINDER SALLY!"

"That I gotta see," said Paul, turning toward the joint.

"No you don't," said Joan, grabbing his arm. "Tomorrow's a long day."

Paul resisted for a moment, then relented.

"You're right. But damn, hate to miss that."

They returned to the boat, and Paul made his eight p.m. call-in. They enjoyed the view from the cockpit with another couple of beers. They rested against the cabin bulkhead looking eastward at the curving sand beach and the lighthouse glowing in the evening sun.

On the eastern horizon of the open lake, a big southbound lake freighter riding low sounded a low single horn blast. The signal was answered by an ocean-going freighter northbound. The single blast from each meant that they would be passing each other port-to-port.

"Probably iron ore bound for Gary or Calumet, and grain for somewhere in Europe," Paul guessed

"Pretty sight," said Joan.

"Yes, great to watch them. But painful to realize now that the world's commercial shipping fleet is one of the major air polluters on the planet. See their long trails of smoke? Virtually no regulations at all for stack emissions. Dirty as hell and full of carbon dioxide. We've got a hell of a long way to go to fix this global warming thing, and way too much political and corporate foot-dragging. There's some positive movement, but nowhere enough yet."

"Your research is helping, isn't it?"

"In its small way. If I can get the plagiarism cleared up so I can publish it."

"Paul, please don't take this the wrong way, because I understand how this sampling trip fits into your overall research, but you have to admit that this sampling series is really very simple and doesn't require any unique equipment. Couldn't people be convinced that Ron could have done the same thing himself?"

"Sure, the field work is simple enough," replied Paul. "But his lab doesn't have the settling chambers to process the phytoplankton samples, and even if it did, the hours required to do the IDs and counting would not have left him time to do his zooplankton work. And more importantly, he couldn't have done the lab experiments I did without our equipment and our algal cultures. Those are the really definitive data that confirm this correlative field work."

"It seems like your lab and his could have made the whole thing into a collaboration with everyone getting authorship."

"That would have been a logical and maybe optimal way to do it. But that may be where Dr. Bates' problem comes in. He has tenure pressure big time, and he needs to be demonstrating independence right now. Publishing with Dr. Perry would not help that. I'm just guessing here; I still don't know if he is directly involved. But Ron Withers knows the situation, and perhaps he is, or was, trying to help Bates on his own."

Joan shuddered. "What a huge stress, the tenure crunch. Makes you think hard about going into academics."

"High risk, high reward, for sure."

Clouds drifted over with a hint of some rain to come, as darkness slowly descended into the harbor. They both retired below, and Paul settled down with a book to wait for his midnight call-in.

# CHAPTER 23

Tuesday, June 29, dawned reluctantly through a veil of overcast drizzle. Paul was stiff all over from yesterday's running; Joan was not. They shivered into jeans, long-sleeved work shirts, and old sweaters. The temperature outside hovered in the upper forties as they microwaved a hearty breakfast of oatmeal and poached eggs. They filled their mugs and thermos with coffee, and made another pot for a second thermos. It would be a long cold day; marine science doesn't wait for sunshine.

In full suits of yellow foul weather gear, Paul and Joan got the shore power cable stowed, brought in the lines, and backed *Tondeleyo* out of the slip. They motored out past Whiskey Point Light in the gray drizzle. There was no wind, so they left the sails furled and throttled up the forty-five horse Detroit Diesel engine to cruising speed.

Paul made his eight a.m. call-in. Station 5 was northeast of them, but Hog Island and the numerous shoals east of it were in their way, and first they had to run due east for sixteen miles to enter Gray's Reef Passage, five miles off Waugashance Point on the mainland. He dialed the channel entrance coordinates into the GPS. It was barely over fifty degrees, and Paul and Joan took turns warming up in the salon. But at least it was a glass smooth ride, and the engine performed flawlessly with little vibration.

Reaching the turning point for the passage at ten-thirty a.m., Paul steered north and kept to the right side of the channel. Visibility wasn't too bad, but Paul had his radar going anyway. These were heavy duty freighter waters; much of the commercial traffic to and from southern Lake Michigan funnels through this narrow passage, and every form of vigilance was imperative. Both Paul and Joan were in the cockpit now, keeping a close watch for both downbound and upbound traffic.

*Tondeleyo* ran the passage uneventfully, and two miles north of the White Shoal Light they reached the sampling station. Station 5 was halfway between Hog Island and Point Aux Chenes on the Upper Peninsula coast. With no wind, Joan did not need to do anything to keep *Tondeleyo* on station, but she kept watch on the radar and scanned the horizon for freighters while Paul did the sampling routine. It was unpleasant in the cold rain, but no hang-ups occurred with the Van Dorn, and they got away by eleven-thirty.

With sandwiches and mugs of coffee from the thermos, they settled into a westerly course for the final Station 6, which was in the middle of the Straits of Mackinac, three miles west of the Mackinac Bridge. As seasoned Michiganders, Paul and Joan pronounced both of these names the original French way, sounding the same as Mackinaw City, where the south end of the bridge begins. Along the way, Paul made his noon call-in.

By three p.m. they were on station. The rain had stopped, and there was a clearing sky inching its way over from the west. Paul hurried the sampling as much as he could, worried as hell about freighters. He had hoisted a radar reflector to the top of the mainmast to increase their visibility on other ships' radar, and he told Joan to shout the instant a ship showed on *Tondeleyo's* radar. At three twenty she said it looked like there was a ship about fifteen miles to the west and coming this way.

"Should leave us enough time, but just barely," said Paul. "Keep an eye on her."

Before taking the final three thermocline-depth samples, Paul got on the VHF channel 16. "SECURITAY, SECURITAY, SECURITAY. This is sail yacht *Tondeleyo* stationary in the water just west of the Mackinac Bridge. Calling freighter eastbound from White Shoal Light. Can you see me on your radar?"

A singsong voice answered immediately. "*Tondeleyo*, dis is motor vessel *Guben Noak*. I see you, yust barely on my screen. Vat are your intentions? Over."

"*Guben Noak*, thank you. After taking water samples here, in about ten minutes I intend to motor to my northwest toward Saint Helena Island. Over."

"Roger dat, *Tondeleyo*. I vill stay to de south of you. *Guben Noak* out."

"Thanks again. *Tondeleyo* out."

"Nice guy," Paul said to Joan. "Swedish, probably."

Paul quickly got back to the sampler to finish up. The freighter was a couple of miles from them as Paul filled the last sample bottle, capped it, and got *Tondeleyo* underway heading north away from the freighter's course. The big blue-hulled salty from Stockholm was giving them plenty of room, but Paul wanted to show good faith, and he didn't want to be anywhere near that behemoth when it plowed through.

The freighter's deep throated horn blew one long and two shorts, the master's salute. Paul only waved back; the ship's captain would never hear *Tondeleyo's* smaller horn while facing away from the ship at that distance. A few minutes later the ship's bow wash started *Tondeleyo* rocking like a bell buoy in a full gale.

"Hang on," said Paul as he turned onto a course for Saint Helena Island, clearly visible to the northwest. *Tondeleyo* settled back down quickly, and Paul made his four p.m. call.

There was some wind now, bringing the clearing skies toward them a bit faster, but they only had a few miles to go, and they didn't bother with the sails for that. As they relaxed for the short run to the island, Joan asked Paul about his radio call to the freighter.

"Why were you saying 'securitay' on the radio back there?"

"It's the French word for security, with an accented 'e' on the end. Maritime tradition, like 'mayday.' That's not 'May day,' as in May first, but rather 'm'aider.'" Paul spelled it out. "That's French for help me. 'Secutitay' is a lower level of alert indicating possible danger."

"Merci," said Joan.

At five p.m. *Tondeleyo* rounded up into the wind in the small bay on the northeast side of the island, which lay a couple of miles off Gros Cap on the Upper Peninsula shore. The bay was sheltered from the prevailing southwest winds, and it was very calm. Paul dropped the anchor in the clear blue-green water, watching it all the way to the bottom fifteen feet below. The light breeze was not enough to get the anchor to take hold in the sand by drifting back, so Paul backed the boat with the engine to accomplish that, and then shut off the engine. They should be set for the night, but Paul programmed the GPS to give a warning beep if the anchor dragged and the boat changed position significantly.

It was turning into a nice evening, and it had actually warmed up into the sixties. Paul and Joan shrugged out of their foul weather gear, and sat down in the cockpit with a couple of cans of Miller to toast the successful sampling run.

They had the bay all to themselves, with a breathtaking view of the uninhabited small island in front of them, the limestone bluffs of Gros Cap behind them, and the "Mighty Mac" Bridge stretching across the horizon in the mist over to the west. But hunger from the long cold day soon got the best of them, and they went below. Paul started the generator so they could quickly heat up some canned corned beef hash and green beans in the microwave. Mundane but satisfying.

After a dessert of chocolate chip cookies, they went back up to the cockpit for a while. At eight PM, Paul doggedly made his scheduled phone call to the institute. The constant reminder of his invisible tether to the criminal justice system was grinding at him more than ever now. He tried to conceal it, but Joan saw through that as clearly as if he had shouted it through a megaphone.

"Wouldn't it be nice if Ron just woke up and said it was all an accident?" said Joan.

"You would see me dancing on top of the water all the way to shore and back." Paul took a deep breath and blew it out between tightly pursed lips, staring at the island. "The chances of that are on the south side of zero, I'm afraid."

"You know, they say that skepticism is a valuable virtue," Joan deadpanned, "...but I doubt it."

That got a chuckle from Paul.

They had intended to make a quick trip ashore before dark, but they were exhausted. Paul switched on the anchor light, and they stumbled below to their bunks. Paul set his wristwatch alarm for midnight for his call-in, and they both fell sound asleep.

# Chapter 24

Wednesday morning, Paul's eight a.m. wristwatch alarm woke him to find *Tondeleyo* straining at her anchor as a twenty knot west wind whined in her rigging. The anchor was holding, but barely so. The bay was still in the lee of the island, but big waves were rolling by only a few hundred feet away over in the channel, and swells were bending around into the bay. Some high fluffy cumulus clouds were racing each other across the pale blue sky. Paul turned on the VHF and listened to the WX weather band. The present conditions were expected to hold for most of the day.

After his call-in, Paul waited for Joan to wake up, which wasn't long because of the boat's motion in the swells. Paul started the generator again and got a coffee pot going, and Joan joined in the breakfast preparation. Paul left the generator running for a while to charge the batteries that were running the refrigerator and the anchor light all night. Up in the cockpit in sweatshirts and windbreakers, second mugs of coffee in hand, they contemplated the day before them.

"Well, Captain, the sampling cruise has been officially completed," said Joan. "What's the plan?"

"We got the sampling done faster than I expected, and it's a little nasty out on the open water today," replied Paul. "I'm thinking let's stay put and explore this island and hope for better traveling weather tomorrow. In the profession, we call it a "lay day."

"Is that so? Uh...something's a little fishy about the terminology there."

Paul shrugged, hands splayed and eyebrows up. "Hey, I don't make 'em up."

"Yeah, but some other sailor did. I know you randy bastards."

"Well how 'bout it? A nice day's hike on solid ground, or a bitch of a beating on the high seas?"

"You're right, it is a no-brainer. But we really will be guilty of skylarking on a perfectly good work day."

"I won't tell the lab pukes if you won't," replied Paul.

Joan went below to pack a lunch and some water bottles in a backpack, and Paul shut off the generator, set a second anchor, and got the dinghy ready in its davits. Paul put the satellite phone in a Velcro pocket, and they shut everything down and locked the hatch. The swells made entering the dinghy an interesting exercise, but except for a couple of banged shins they got away okay and rowed for the sand beach.

Saint Helena was a windswept, low-lying limestone island about a mile long, with the unique flora typical of the northern Great Lakes islands. After pulling the dinghy up on the beach, Paul and Joan started walking southeast along the shore beside the beach grasses. Spindly-legged sandpipers comically patrolled and pecked along the shoreline ahead of them.

Turning up off the beach, Paul and Joan entered a meadow that was riotous in the bright reds of the columbines, deep blues of the dwarf lake irises, and pinks of the pitcher's thistles, all of which were quaking violently on their short stems in the stiff wind as though they were jiggling in the back of a wagon on a cobblestone street. Further along, at the edge of a shrub-land of leather leaf and Labrador tea, Paul and Joan found a carpet of small, tart, wild strawberries that kept them busy for a while.

Moving on, they walked back over to the beach to skirt around a thick grove of cedar and hemlock trees, not as tall as they would have been had they not grown in this exposed environment. Nearing the southeast end of the island, an abandoned light house came into view. It looked like it needed exploring, and Joan and Paul headed for it. The faded brick tower was inviting, but its entrance was within the attached brick lighthouse keeper's bungalow. They walked around to the front door of the house, still decorated by old lilac bushes and bright orange day lilies. There was no lock on the door, and it squeaked opened when Paul pushed on it. They looked at each other, shrugged and went in.

At the other end of the empty ground floor, there was a big rusty lock on the door to the light tower. Bummer. So instead they climbed the dusty stairs of the house to see the view from the second floor. As they reached the top of the stairs, several pigeons exploded away out of the pane-less front window, startling Joan so badly that she nearly fell back down the stairs.

There were two dilapidated rooms, both empty except for several old musty mattresses scattered around the floors, and some empty beer cans and other evidence of recent activity, most likely high school kids from nearby St. Ignace or Mackinaw City. Paul gazed at one of the mattresses for a long moment, and then over at Joan. Joan looked back, saw his half grin, and her eyes suddenly got real big.

"Oh no," she said, heading for the stairs. "I'm out of here."

She ran down, and he walked down after her. He now had a full grin. Joan went out the front door and trotted all the way over to the south-facing beach. Paul caught up, and they sat down to rest and view the panorama of the Straits before them. There were flat, wave-worn stones here that were warm in the sun, and soon Joan and Paul were both relaxing on their backs, eyes closed against the bright sunshine.

Paul had just started to doze, when suddenly he felt Joan reach across him and pull herself on top of him. Very soon there was a frantic fumbling of hands clutching at zippers and buttons as though every article of clothing was on fire. Breathing grew deeper, and louder, and faster, until it sounded as though a pair of racing thoroughbreds were approaching, pounding, thundering on by and then fading, whispering away in the distance.

As they untangled and got side by side again on their backs, they were startled by a long and two short horn blasts from a freighter passing close to the island.

Paul raised up on his elbows. "We just got saluted."

"What do you mean?"

"There's no other ship in sight. That was for us." Paul raised his arm and waved the thumbs up sign.

"Oh stop, Paul"

The horn sounded again.

"See?" Paul grinned.

"Oh god. So how many sailors do suppose were watching us?"

"Well, all of the deck apes are below playing euchre or sleeping. But the officer on watch in the pilothouse is probably putting the binocs back in the rack right about now."

"Good god." Joan shook a middle finger salute at the ship. "That's just in case the slime ball is still watching. Paul, you've been here before, haven't you? You planned this whole thing, you sneak."

"Scout's honor Joan, I've seen it several times from the water sailing by with Kerrigan, but never set foot on it before. Always wanted to, though. So, well...half guilty, your honor."

Joan laughed, and settled down on her back to finish catching her breath. Paul did the same. They held hands there for a half hour, and then Paul thought to look at his watch.

"Oops, the noon call time blew right by, back there. Must not have heard the alarm."

"You wouldn't have heard a nuclear bomb."

They got up and started walking back northwestward along the outer beach. Paul made the call.

"Dave, Paul here. Yeah, we're still here on St. Helena. Weather's for shit and we're taking a lay day." He winked at Joan. She punched him in the shoulder. "Ouch! What? Oh. I, uh, stubbed my toe on a beach rock. Anyway, if the wind drops, we'll start for home tomorrow. Anything new? Okay. Talk to you at four."

Paul and Joan walked on for a half mile or so and then stopped on the beach to eat their sandwiches. The wind showed no sign of letting up, but it was not expected to drop until evening. Here on the windward side, it was glorious but hardly relaxing. The beach grass was lying flat on the ground from the constant wind. Gulls and terns wheeled and bleated continually, just audible in the roar of the surf piling in from across the north end of Lake Michigan.

In a while, they got up and continued their walk around the perimeter of the island, and at one-thirty they arrived back at the dinghy. In went the backpack, and they shoved off. The wind pushed them rapidly across the swells on the blue bay to where *Tondeleyo* lay, nosing back and forth on her tether like a nervous mare. Another mad scramble at the stern, and they were back aboard. After hoisting the dinghy on its davits, they dozed in the sun on the cockpit seats out of the wind. Soon they fell into full-fledged naps.

When Paul and Joan woke up later in the afternoon, the wind had started backing around into the south and slowing down, with a hint of warmer weather to come. The sun was still high in the west. Paul looked at his watch and said, "It's beer-thirty."

"Sun's not below the yard arm, Captain," Joan pretended to complain.

"Will be when I raise the yard arm."

He went below, visited the head, and brought up a couple of cold ones and some cheese and crackers. Joan made a pit stop below too, and then joined Paul back in the cockpit. Paul leaned back against the mizzen mast and watched the top of the main mast draw lazy arcs in the cobalt sky.

"Times like this I can't help quoting my late mentor Ian. 'Wonder what the poor people are doing this afternoon.'"

"Not funny Paul. You should leave that one in the grave with him. Besides, that prosecutor gets his way, you'll get real educated about what they're doing, every day."

"Got a point there."

Paul made is four p.m. call.

Afternoon wore on into evening, with a late dinner in the cockpit framed by a flaming sunset that filled half the western sky. It had become very calm and comfortably warm. A few hands of rummy down at the settee after dark, and it was sack time. Tomorrow should be a fine sailing day. Paul had one last comment as he stretched and yawned in his bunk.

"Still wish I'd seen Sidewinder Sally back on Beaver Island."

Joan ignored him and fell asleep.

# Chapter 25

Thursday, July 1, Joan and Paul were up early, and with the engine idling they eased *Tondeleyo* up over the anchors and raised them. They motored out of the bay, set sail, fell away onto a southwesterly course and shut off the engine. They were headed for Gray's Reef Passage, close-hauled in the ten knot south wind. They would be able to make the entrance to the passage by shortly after noon under these conditions, but if the wind stayed in the south, they would then have to use the engine, as their course was nearly due south from there. Tacking through the narrow passage was out of the question, and they wanted to get back to Elk Rapids as soon as possible.

They were having a nice sail. It was warm and sunny, and no tacking was needed. At eight a.m. Paul made his call-in, but this time no one answered the call.

"No answer," said Paul. "That's weird."

They sailed on, and ten minutes later Paul tried the call again.

"Still no answer. Something's wrong."

They sailed further on in silence.

At ten-twenty, Paul started to reach for the phone yet again when it rang. Paul jerked back his hand and stared hard at the phone. On the third ring he finally picked it up and opened it.

"Paul? This is Craig."

Paul's vision got a little blurry. "Yeah Craig. You're calling on RULI's sat phone, right?"

"Paul, I hope you are sitting down."

"Craig, cut the shit. What have you got?"

"Withers went brain dead last night. They're pulling the plug today."

Paul drew a deep breath and looked skyward.

"It gets worse," continued Craig. "Prosecutor's pissed that you're way up there, but he's willing to overlook that if you get your ass into Mackinaw City ASAP so the police can run you back down here. He's upping the charge to murder one."

Paul was silent for a moment. He turned to Joan, noticing her white knuckled grip on the wheel. "Ron's dead, and it's murder one now," Paul told her. She looked away to the horizon.

Paul turned back to the phone. "Craig, I don't see why we can't just motor straight on down there. We're on our way now."

"That won't fly, I'm afraid. I tried like hell to get that to happen, but the guy is on the warpath here. We're lucky he isn't ordering a helicopter pickup out there."

"So what happens when I get into Mackinaw?"

"Officers are on their way there now in a county cruiser. You are to meet them at the marina dock."

"What do I do with Joan and my boat?"

"They're letting you figure that out for yourself, I'm afraid. Is there some way I can help with that?"

"Not at the moment. I'll figure something out."

"Paul, this change doesn't make their fundamental case any stronger, and I still think it's pretty thin. But we are obviously getting into more dangerous water here, and I've asked a friend of mine in criminal law to work with us. Is that okay with you?"

"Sure, yeah. Go ahead and circle the wagons, Craig. Look, I've got to change course here. I'll be in touch. Thanks for brightening up my day. Ciao."

Paul and Joan brought the boat around to a port tack, close reaching on an easterly course. Paul started the engine and gave it just enough throttle to kick *Tondeleyo* on up to her full cruising speed. Then Paul dialed Dave Washington at RULI, and this time Washington answered.

"Dave, I guess you know the score. I'm hauling ass for Mackinaw City; should get in at about one-thirty. Cops will have me in Traverse by late afternoon, I imagine. I hope Dr. Tollefson isn't in a bind over this."

"Not so far. Let's hope it stays that way. You're the one we are worried about though."

"Thanks Dave. Talk to you later."

Paul closed the phone and turned to Joan. "So what in hell do we do with you and the boat?"

"Can you get someone to help me take it back to Elk Rapids?"

"I don't know who I could get from down there, but maybe Marty McAllister can come up with something." Paul dialed McAllister, and explained the legal bind he was in and the problem with Joan and the boat. "Do you know anyone who could come up and help Joan bring the boat back home?"

"I'll do it meself, son. Me dock hand can drive me up, and the wife kin mind the store. It's not so's we're overlooaded with work these days. Them damn big marinas, ye know."

"Look Marty, just rent a car – I'll pay for it"

"Don't be silly son. I'll be at the dock. Take care now."

"Marty, I don't know how to thank you. See you in a few hours."

Paul closed the phone and told Joan she was going to ship out with one of the finest sailors on the Great Lakes.

"Too bad I won't be able to enjoy it under the circumstances," Joan replied. "But we'll get *Tondeleyo* back in one piece. You'd better give me your car keys so I can run him back up to Charlevoix and then get down to Traverse."

"Good idea."

They lapsed into silence as *Tondeleyo* plowed along. The weather continued to be gorgeous, but it went unnoticed by Joan and Paul. Twice during the three hour run, a police helicopter clattered over them, obviously checking on their heading and progress before circling back to Mackinaw City. Paul gave it a look he would have given a vulture circling over him in the desert.

# CHAPTER 26

At one forty-five, *Tondeleyo* eased up to the fuel dock at the Mackinaw City Municipal Marina. On the dock stood Martin McAllister and a uniformed officer, each ferociously ignoring the other. Thumbs in his belt, the officer rocked on his heels and watched Marty help tie up the boat. Paul directed the attendant to top off the diesel tank, and stepped ashore with a sea bag.

Shaking Marty's hand, Paul said "I've got the courses to Elk Rapids all plotted in the GPS, Marty."

"Ach. Don't need that, son. Do it with me eyes cloosed."

"I know. Take care of Joan. She's a treasure."

"She'll be takin' care o' me, I'm thinkin'. Fine strong lass."

"That she is."

Joan stepped ashore and gave Paul a long hard hug. "Keep your chin up, sailor boy. I'll see you as soon as I can."

"Bye Joan."

Paul turned and trudged toward the officer. Only then did Paul recognize the man as "Officer 23" who had fed him to the toughs in the drunk tank. Apparently not amused by all the emotional dallying, the cop scowled as though he had just stepped in dog shit with his best shoes.

After rummaging through Paul's sea bag as though it was certain to contain several lethal weapons, the cop led Paul to the cruiser where a backup officer was leaning against the door. They slapped a pair of cuffs on Paul so tight his hands turned purple immediately. There was no conversation whatsoever as they headed south toward Traverse City. Officer 23 did not use the flashers, but he drove very fast.

After paying for the fuel, Joan helped Martin aboard *Tondeleyo* with his sea bag. Martin started the engine, and Joan cast off. Motoring out of the harbor, Martin asked Joan if she had ever made an overnight passage at sea. She had not.
"Fine time to start," Martin said. "We'll be standin' watches four on an' four off. Ye'll take the firrst watch. That way it'll be me takin' her through the Reef Passage. After that, she's a milk run straight down to Elk Rapids."
Martin turned *Tondeleyo* into the wind, and Joan got the sails up. Coming onto a broad reach westward under the Macinac Bridge, Martin throttled the engine up to achieve cruising speed, and turned the wheel over to Joan.
"I'll be takin' me nap now, lass. Give me a holler when that silly GPS thing says we're comin' onto the Passage markers. Or sooner if the wind shifts. And be watchin' fer them big boys."
"Gotcha, skipper."
A few hours later they turned south into Gray's Reef Passage. Joan and Martin took in *Tondeleyo's* sails and motored directly into the moderate south wind all through the night. Continuing to work watch-and-watch (four on, four off), it was taking all of Friday to complete the trip down to Elk Rapids.

Paul was spending the day with Craig Basham, getting through the new arraignment for murder. Craig introduced Paul to Harold Holmes, his criminal law friend who had agreed to help them with the defense.

"Hope you take plastic, Mr. Holmes," said Paul while shaking hands.

"Call me Hal, and forget the plastic, Paul. Some sailing lessons for my son and daughter will do fine."

"You're not serious."

"Yes I am."

"Deal."

At the arraignment they learned that Paul's fingerprints had been found on the hatch cover. No surprise. Dozens of people including Paul entered that hold from time to time. They also learned that Larry Griffin had told the prosecutor that he saw Paul follow Ron Withers below that morning. This was devastating. The tardiness of Griffin's declaration might cause some trouble for the prosecutor, but they knew he would play this new ammunition it for all it was worth. A grand jury hearing was scheduled for Monday morning.

After the arraignment, Paul was allowed to leave the courthouse but was required to remain strictly within the Traverse City limits. To ensure that he did so, he was fitted with an ankle collar that transmitted his location to police headquarters.

At two-thirty p.m., Craig drove Paul over to the institute where Paul used the satellite phone to call Joan on *Tondeleyo*. He told her the situation and learned that the boat would arrive in Elk Rapids around eight p.m.

"How's it going with the gnarly old Scotsman?"

"Very well, Paul. This round-the-clock watch-and-watch sea passage stuff is quite something. I'm ready for a trans-Atlantic."

"I'll put that on the schedule. Prosecutor'll love the idea. Look Joan, if you're too tired, don't try to drive Martin home tonight."

"It's only about thirty-five miles from Elk Rapids to Charlevoix, but we'll see how it goes."

"I'll be staying at Craig's. Call me on my cell phone when you get in to Elk Rapids, okay?"

"Yes Paul. Bye."

Paul spent the rest of the afternoon doing odds and ends in the lab, and at five-thirty Craig picked him up and they drove toward Craig's home. The streets were gridlocked.

"What's all the traffic about?" said Paul.

"Cherry Festival, dude."

"Oh, of course. Might as well be in Detroit or Chicago."

"This is only the beginning."

"Oh Lord. It goes on for days, doesn't it?"

"Yep."

They finally broke free and made it the few blocks to Craig's place. After a pleasant dinner with Craig and his wife, Paul watched television until Joan called at nine fifteen. They were in Elk Rapids, but she was too tired to drive Martin to Charlevoix that night.

"I'll drive him in the morning, and get back to Traverse City sometime before noon, okay?"

"Yep. Have a good sleep, Joan."

"You too, if you can. Are you okay?"

"Just ducky." Paul reconsidered the sarcasm. "Yes, I really am okay. See you tomorrow."

Paul was exhausted, and fell right to sleep in Craig's guest room bed.

Saturday morning Joan loaded Paul's equipment and samples into his Mustang and drove Martin McAllister up to Charlevoix. She was approaching Traverse City by ten a.m., but festival traffic brought her to a crawl. Detouring south around the airport, she finally got to Craig's at eleven.

Craig's wife directed Joan out to the back deck where Paul and Craig were having coffee. Paul rose and hugged Joan, and Craig shook her hand.

"How's our sailor girl?" asked Craig. "I hear you're qualified for your mate's ticket."

"Don't know about that, but I think I'm ready for the Chicago to Mackinaw race."

"You know," said Paul, "that's a hell of an idea. Let's plan on that next summer."

"Well," said Craig, "if we can get you through *this* summer, I'm in."

"Right now, I am desperately in need of a shower, as you maybe can tell," said Joan.

Paul drained the last of his coffee and said, "Let's go, Anne Bonny."

"Who's that?" said Joan.

"Famous eighteenth century woman pirate. Fearless. Took no prisoners."

"Good for her," said Joan as she took Paul's hand and headed for his car.

Driving to Joan's apartment took forty-five minutes; the traffic was still terrible. Joan took a long hot shower while Paul surfed through her cable TV channels.

After lunch at a deli across the street, Paul and Joan drove the Mustang to the institute and brought the equipment and sample boxes into the Perry lab. Dr. Perry was there, and he stared at Paul's ankle collar for a moment.

"How are you doing, Paul?"

"Well, I'm beginning to understand how Emperor Hirohito felt in August of Nineteen Forty-five when he said, 'The war situation has developed not necessarily to Japan's advantage.'"

Perry smiled briefly but looked again at Paul's ankle collar.

Paul set up the two settling chamber rigs, gently shook the first dozen sample bottles to get the plankton well mixed, and filled the chamber columns. No time like the present to get started with the long ID and counting process. What else was he going to do while waiting for the proverbial wheels of justice to grind along?

Joan went to her lab to get started catching up on her own research. When it was time to leave for the day, they decided to leave the Mustang in the institute lot and walk to her apartment. Festival traffic was impossible now.

With hardly enough room for two to live in Joan's apartment ("I have to go out in the hall to change my mind," she often said), Paul continued to stay in Craig Basham's guest room at night. He missed being on the boat, but Craig's hospitality was very welcome. With the Grand Jury looming, there was little enthusiasm for attending any of the Cherry Festival activities, and on Sunday Paul and Joan spent the day in the lab again.

Late in the afternoon, they did cave in and buy a fresh cherry pie from a street vendor on the walk back to Joan's apartment. It livened up Joan's simple dinner. They watched some lousy TV, and Paul walked back to Craig's and went to bed early.

Before long Paul was embroiled in a harrowing dream. Officer 23 and a posse of hundreds were chasing Paul through a cedar swamp with rifles and cannons blazing away. He fought toward waking up, drenched in sweat and breathing hard, but the cannons were still firing. Finally he was fully awake. More cannons. *What the hell?* It finally dawned on him; the Fourth of July fireworks were underway just offshore in the West Arm. They pounded away for another twenty minutes, and then Paul fell back to sleep.

# CHAPTER 27

On Monday morning, July 5, Paul and Joan were sitting nervously with the new Basham and Holmes defense team in the lobby outside the grand jury room at the courthouse. Although they would not be allowed inside for the proceedings, they wanted to see who was being brought in to testify. At nine a.m. the prosecutor strode by and into the room. Soon after, the parade of witnesses went in, including the county marine inspector, then one of the forensic technicians, followed by Dr. Bates, and finally Larry Griffin. Bates looked embarrassed. Griffin looked smug.

"I don't know if Larry Griffin is doing this just to spite Joan and me, or if he's got a deal going with Bates now," said Paul.

"If this goes to court," said Craig, "we'll have to bring Joan in to testify about Griffin's threat to her."

Joan groaned. Holmes nodded and said, "It will be rough going. He-said-she-said testimony stands up about like Jell-O in a microwave."

"Still gotta do it," said Craig. "Anyway, we might as well head back to my office to wait for the news. The coffee is better there."

The decision of the grand jury was in just before noon. Paul was indicted for first degree murder. The trial was scheduled for the Monday of August 2.

The local press and TV made note of the indictment in its coverage of the case of "violence on the high seas of Lake Michigan," and a Detroit Free Press reporter arrived in town to sniff around the story. But virtually no one had noticed another development that was unfolding nearby at the county jail during Paul's grand jury proceedings. That morning, two men were being released eight days early from a thirty day stay in jail for drunk and disorderly conduct and public urination. Their names were Jake Fenner and Arthur Kopke. Jake and Arty were the toughs that Paul had tangled with in the drunk tank on that dark Saturday when all hell broke loose.

Paul's nemesis, "Office 23," escorted the two men out to the main lobby. As Jake turned to shake hands with the officer, he winced and grabbed the side of his chest in pain.

"Those ribs still sore?" asked Officer 23.

"That son of a bitch broke three of 'em," said Jake. "They're still taped. I need to find out who he is. Make the fucker pay."

Officer 23 nodded slowly and then broke into a grin as though something had come to mind. He glanced around the empty lobby and then spoke softly.

"I might be able to help. Let's go outside."

Out in the back parking lot Officer 23 once again looked around to make sure he wasn't being observed talking with the two men.

"His name is Paul Tyson. He's a student over at the university water institute, or whatever it's called. I don't know much about him, but he's in trouble up to his ass – probably being indicted for murder right now over in the courthouse. Supposed to have fatally assaulted another student on one of the research boats earlier in the day that he fucked you two up."

"Figures," said Jake. "I still want a piece of him. How do I learn more?"

The officer replied, "You didn't hear this from me, but another student named Larry Griffin seems to be interested in fucking Tyson up too. He's giving the prosecutor some juicy shit to use in the trial. He might be willing to give you some useful information. But if I hear that you used my name in this, I will make things very difficult for you next time you're in here.

"Paul Tyson. Larry Griffin. Remember those names, Arty," said Jake.

"Sure as hell," replied Arthur, who was still sore himself from Paul's groin kick back on that day in the drunk tank. He wouldn't be engaging in any sexual activity for a while.

Jake and Arty thanked Officer 23 and walked a few blocks to a locals' bar for their first beers since June 12. Being dry for that long was worse than their injuries, and they had a lot of catching up to do. After slamming the first two glasses of cheap draft, Jake called his younger brother and told him to bring him his truck.

An hour and several beers later, Jake's rusty white F150 pickup pulled up outside the bar and idled loudly while Jake and Arty paid their tab. Jake took his seat behind the wheel, and his brother squeezed over between him and Arty on the bench seat. They drove over onto U.S. 31 and entered the institute parking lot. Jake parked, found the institute entrance sign on the limnology building and walked into the office.

"I'm looking for Larry Griffith," Jake said to the secretary behind the counter.

"Um, you mean Larry Griffin?"

"Yeah, Griffin"

"Larry works in Dr. Bates' lab."

"Where would that be?"

The secretary pointed to the directory on the wall behind Jake.

"Room 1057, down that hall and to the right," she said.

"Thanks sweetie pie."

The secretary glared at Jake as he turned for the door.
"Creep," she muttered at her computer screen.

Jake walked right in to Dr. Bates' lab. Griffin was the only one in the lab.
"You Larry Griffith?"
"It's Griffin. Who are you?"
"Name's Jake. I'm told you can tell me some things about Paul Tylon."
"You mean Paul Tyson?"
"Yeah, Tyson."
Griffin sized up this scruffy lout who smelled like a back street beer dive. The guy had trouble written all over him. But maybe he presented an interesting opportunity.
"Look," said Griffin, "First of all, don't ever come in here again. Now go out the side door down the hall that way, and drive over to the marina parking lot. I'll meet you there in a few minutes."
Jake did as he was told. Griffin waited a few minutes, then walked out the side entrance to his car. He drove the few hundred yards west on U.S. 31 and into the marina parking lot. He saw Jake and the two others, and parked as far as he could from the truck. He pointed over at the beach to the west of the lot and walked that way. Jake followed him out along the beach in front of the empty volleyball courts.
"What's this all about?" asked Griffin.
"Got a score to settle with Tyson. Need to know where he lives, what he drives, like that."
Griffin digested that. *Score to settle, eh?*
"What do you have in mind?"
"Don't know yet, but we'll think of something"
"We?"
"Arty in the truck there's got a score to settle too."
Griffin began to get the picture. He remembered hearing about the drunk tank scuffle.
"Oh, you're the guys…"

Jake cut him off. "Never mind, dude. What can you tell me?"

"Okay, I'll tell you this. Tyson lives on a black-hulled sailboat named *Tondeleyo* in the Elk Rapids harbor. He drives an old red mustang. It's in the institute lot right now; he can't leave Traverse City."

"But you said he lives in Elk Rapids."

"Not right now. He's staying at his lawyer's place. I don't know where that is."

"Beautiful," said Jake.

"Don't ever link me to you or your friend, or I'll rat you out big time."

"You got it dude. Like they say, this conversation never happened."

Griffin nodded and watched Jake walk back to the lot, get in his truck and drive out. As Larry walked to his car, he could hear Jake's straight pipes roaring like a rocket launch long after the truck was out of sight.

Approaching the institute, Jake slowed down and eyeballed Paul's Mustang in the lot. He looked at his brother and Arty.

"There a hardware store in Elk Rapids?"

"Probably," said Arty.

"Need some tools," said Jake as he picked up speed on northbound U.S. 31.

# Chapter 28

During the week after the indictment, Paul and Joan took a break from lab work and spent some time strolling around town taking in some of the Cherry Festival. In spite of their lousy mood, they found themselves amazed by the air show, and they enjoyed several other events.

But by Saturday, July 10, they were thoroughly sick of the traffic and the crowds, and they were glad there was only one more day of Festival left. Mid-morning they were walking from a coffee shop on Front Street toward Joan's apartment when a loud white pickup truck rumbled around the corner from a side street and suddenly stopped beside them. The driver and the passenger jumped out of the cab and stalked over in front of Paul and Joan. It took Paul a microsecond to recognize Jake and Arty, though he did not know their names.

"Well if it ain't the pretty boy college puke," said Arty.

Paul stared at both men, a sneer curling at his lips.

"You shitheads back for more?"

Jake stepped toward Paul with a balled fist, but Arty grabbed Jake.

"Jake, don't forget your ribs. They ain't ready. You'll get one through your lung."

Jake halted.

"Okay Arty, you're right. It can wait." But Jake kept staring at Paul.

"Tyson, we mighta been a little careless back in round one, but we've only begun. You and your bitch get on your way now, hear?"

Paul started for Jake, but Joan held him back.

"Paul, this is the last thing you need right now."

Paul stared at Jake. "How do you know my name, shithead?"

"Friends in high places, dude," replied Jake. "C'mon Arty."

The men returned to the truck and slowly rumbled off down the street. Paul stared long and hard after them.

"Those were the drunk tank guys, weren't they?" asked Joan.

"Yes."

"Will they come after you again?"

"Perhaps. Probably. But something's wrong. They know who I am. What else do they know?"

Paul thought for a minute. Then he yanked his cell phone out of his pocket and punched up a stored number.

"Craig. Yeah, it's me. Are you tied up right now? Listen, I just had a run-in with those two drunks from the jail cell. No, they're still too busted up to actually fight yet, but Craig, they know some things. They know my name. How? What else do they know? I'm thinking somebody like Officer 23 is feeding them info just to see what kind of fun might crop up."

Paul listened for a minute to Craig, who was trying to convince Paul that he was over-reacting a bit. Then Paul's uneasiness shifted from vague wondering to stark premonition.

"Craig. Can you get out to my boat ASAP? I need to check on it, but of course I can't leave town. You can do that? Great."

Joan grabbed the phone from Paul.

"Craig, pick me up at my apartment on your way. Thanks."

"No way," said Paul.

"Paul, I'm going out there. You wait at my place."

Paul nodded reluctantly. "Damn this fucking ankle collar."

Craig and Joan pulled into the Elk Rapids marina lot and walked toward Paul's boat. They could hear trouble before they got to her. All three of *Tondeleyo's* bilge pump outflow ports were gushing water into the harbor. Closer to the boat they could see why. A white water hose from the dock tap was snaked across the deck into the cockpit and down into the salon. The lock on the hatch had been broken with a bolt cutter. The hose was running full force.

"Jesus Christ," said Craig.

Joan smoldered with hands on her hips. "Those bastards." She shut off the tap and pulled the hose out of the hatch. They both descended the ladder into the salon, afraid of what they would find down there.

"Holy mackerel," said Craig. "Paul is lucky. The deck is awash down here, but it's all going down that drain into the bilge. They were trying to sink the boat."

"The idiots didn't know about the bilge pumps," said Joan. "Or else they figured the batteries would wear down. But Paul has an automatic battery charger. Thank heavens Marty and I stayed aboard last Friday night, or I might have neglected to connect the shore power when we arrived."

Craig gave Joan a look. "Uh, who is Marty, Joan?"

"Oh for crying out loud. Martin McAllister, remember? Paul's Charlevoix friend who brought the boat back with me from Mackinaw?"

"Oh yeah, sure."

"Using Paul's boat for random trysts is an interesting idea, but it's not my style."

"Of course not. Sorry Joan. I lost track a bit, what with my focus on the trial."

"That's okay. You just keep focusing on that trial like a laser, counselor. Let's call Paul with this lovely bit of news."

Joan dialed her apartment on her cell phone and told Paul what they had found. Sitting on the edge of her day bed, Paul gave the mattress a punch with his fist.

"We've got to move the boat. Stay there while I call Dave Washington. I'll call you back in a minute."

Paul dialed the institute headquarters.

"This is Paul Tyson. Get me Dave Washington please."

"Hi Paul."

"Dave, I've got more problems. Those two drunks I beat up in jail last month are out and have started to retaliate. They tried to sink my boat with a deck hose. Fortunately they're too stupid to know about bilge pumps or automatic battery chargers. But I've got to move the boat to a safe place. The only thing I can think of right now is RULI harbor where we can all keep an eye on her. Is there any chance of that, at least temporarily?"

Washington thought a minute. "Yeah, I think we could do that, at least for a while. Personal boats in the harbor are against policy, as you well know, but this is a special case. You can tie up along the inner side of the sea wall, forward of the *Chinook*." The *Chinook* was the 35-foot lobsterman.

"Thanks a million Dave."

Paul dialed Joan. "We can put her in RULI harbor for now. Can you and Crag get her down here? It would take all afternoon even under power, but you could get here before dark."

Joan held the phone and conferred with Craig. Back on the phone she told Paul they could do it.

"Great," said Paul. "I'll walk over to the lab for the afternoon. Call me when you're fifteen minutes out, and I'll be out there to show you where Dave wants her. You're a sweetheart, and Craig's a prince."

Joan closed the phone and went below to find a sponge and a bucket to dry off the teak-and-holly cabin sole. Craig coiled the water hose and hung it up on its pedestal hook on the dock. He unplugged the shore power and coiled the cable on the deck. Then he started the engine to warm it up, took in most of the mooring lines, and waited for Joan to finish down below. They would be motoring in a moderate chop under partly cloudy skies, up around Mission Point and back down the West Arm.

When Paul got to the institute, he went straight to his Mustang in the parking lot. He walked around it slowly, and found no obvious signs of vandalism. He opened the hood and found everything okay under there; no bomb, no stolen distributor. He crawled under the car and scanned the underside. He found no bomb there either, and the brake lines had not been cut. *So far, so good, I guess.* Still, he moved the car over right next to his building in view of the main office. He went into the office and asked everyone to keep an eye on his car as best they could. A secretary followed Paul back into the hallway.

"Paul, there was a creep in here the other day looking for Larry Griffin. I didn't think much about it at the time."

"Long dark oily hair, Harley tee shirt?"

"Yeah. I'm sorry Paul."

"That's okay, Mary." *So that's it. That bastard cop hooked the goons up with Griffin.*

Paul went out of his way to walk by the Bates lab. He paused at the open door. Griffin was there and looked at Paul with a smirk. Paul fought back the urge to go in after Griffin, and just nodded as though he knew exactly what was going on. Paul walked back up the hall to Dr. Perry's lab and got busy washing glassware to pass the time while his boat was en route.

At 6:30 p.m. Paul got a call from Joan. "The harbor is in sight. See you soon."

"Ten four, Joan."

Paul walked out to the docks and stood on the sea wall where *Tondeleyo* was to tie up. He watched his boat approach and enter the harbor. Joan did a nice job of rounding up past the lobsterman and stopping her next to Paul without bumping the sea wall. Paul nodded his appreciation and took a line from Craig. Paul secured the rest of the lines while Craig and Joan hung the fenders. After hooking up the shore power Paul tried to thank Craig and Joan profusely, but they waved him off.

"Hey, we're all in this thing, Paul," said Craig. "Just glad we can help."

Joan said "I'm starved. Let's get some dinner somewhere, and then I'll drive Craig back to his car in Elk Rapids."

They headed for the parking lot.

# CHAPTER 29

As the next three weeks wore on, there was little for Paul and Joan to do but slog away in their labs, trying to make some progress in the face of the relentless stress of waiting for the trial. They did improve their moods when they got in the habit of running several miles every day in the late afternoon, either out along the bay on U.S. 31 or at the university track. There was no sign of the rusty white F150 truck.

Paul rapidly improved from his out-of-shape performance back on Beaver Island, and soon he was capable of sustaining the same strong, bounding pace that Joan had been running with for years. But just as the trial was receding into the background of their thoughts, Paul's locator collar started chafing and raising a blister on his ankle. Taping it down for the next day's run, Paul said, "I hope the bastard monitoring this damn thing gets real dizzy when I'm running."

In the lab, Paul plotted out the data from the multi parameter probe that he had collected on *Tondeleyo* and compared them with the corresponding data from the same month the year before. Sure enough, the average temperature of the epilimnion was another degree warmer at all stations than it was at the same time last year. The carbon dioxide content was about ten percent higher, and correspondingly the pH was a tenth of a point lower than last year. A tenth of a pH unit wouldn't sound like much to a lay person, but on the log scale of the pH value, it was a significant change.

Agreement among replicate samples was excellent, showing that the data were highly reliable. All of this was more evidence of the effects of the continuing buildup of carbon dioxide and heat in the atmosphere.

Turning his attention to the phytoplankton samples, Paul scanned slide after slide under the microscope, each slide taking a whole day to count enough fields of view that the counts of each species were accurate to within the ninety-five percent confidence interval. Many of the same newly abundant species from last year were still dominant, and there were three more species that had been rare in the past but now were becoming more common. Paul would have to try to culture those and run the experiments to confirm that the temperature and pH conditions were the driving factors for them, as he had shown for the other species. *Wouldn't Withers have loved to get his hands on these data!* Paul felt a little guilty at that thought; the poor guy was dead after all, and his family must be grieving deeply.

Another slide, another hour, another day, another week. This part of doing science was tedious but necessary. Paul was generating important information for the war on global warming.

Unfortunately, the Bates lab was just down the hall from the Perry lab, and Larry Griffin was still serving his rotation with Dr. Bates. Paul saw Griffin frequently. More than once, when passing each other in the hall, Griffin would smirk like a middle school kid and say, "Hey jailbird." But try as he might, Griffin was unable to get a rise out of Paul. With his temper now firmly under control, Paul just looked at Griffin with the disgust he would show a mangy dog and walked on by.

Paul wondered if the prosecutor was coaching Griffin to provoke Paul into some violence to deepen the hole he was in. It wasn't going to happen.

Craig Basham and Hal Holmes spent some hours with Joan going over what they would ask her on the stand. She would have to relive that disgusting Saturday night with Larry Griffin and reveal to the courtroom her stupidity in letting things go that far. But they had to get Griffin's threat to Joan out in front of the jury so that they would question his credibility. Craig and Harold were not very confident that this would get them much traction, but anything that might instill a reasonable doubt among the jury was worth a carefully aimed shot.

In addition to her research activities, Joan got a welcome distraction from Paul's situation by starting her teaching assistant duties in an introductory biology course for the university's late summer session. Several days before classes began, she got out her notes for the introductory lab presentations from the winter semester, which had been her first time as a TA in that course, and spent some time sprucing them up so that she could give more polished lectures. She attended a couple of TA meetings with the intro lab coordinator who described a couple of new demonstrations and experiments she had developed during the spring.

Joan had two lab sections that each met twice a week, and very soon the grading of weekly quizzes and reports kept her very busy. Her lab sections were full to capacity, and she had a number of students clamoring to be added in to her sections, not only because they were trying to avoid foreign TAs whose English wasn't so good, but also because Joan already had a reputation as being especially good even among the American TAs. Paul had a different hypothesis. "The ones on the waiting list are mostly guys, right? How often do they get a hot babe up in front of the class?"

"Oh right, Paul."

"Trust me on that. Just try keeping track of how often the guys raise their hands for you to come over for some help. Then see if they are actually listening."

Dr. Perry's days continued with nearly normal routine. It hardly fit the lay public's limited movie images of the tweedy professor languorously pontificating to eager undergrads, strolling ivied quadrangles and relaxing in the faculty club debating the number of angels that could fit on the head of a pin. Those images may have been close to the mark for some small liberal arts colleges, but they were a very incomplete glimpse of a professor's life at a major research university.

There were the teaching duties of course, including a number of hours with troubled undergrads unhappy with their grades. But, as at most major research universities, formal classroom teaching occupied a relatively small part of Perry's time. In the mentoring of graduate students, there were countless more hours riding herd on inexperienced students in the lab. New graduate students, in addition to their formal course work and studying for qualifying exams, had to learn new research techniques in the lab, usually by helping the more senior grads. The youngsters had to be monitored to avoid making mistakes that jeopardized the quality of the data or that were dangerous. Most difficult was getting the young grads into a frame of mind of developing their own scientific questions, hypotheses, and strategies.

Perry spent still more hours writing, revising and resubmitting research articles for publication, the principal product of scholarship. To continue securing outside funding to pay for the research, even more hours were needed for writing and revising and resubmitting grant proposals. External funding was by far the largest criterion for advancement in tenure and promotion. In between these, there was reviewing journal manuscripts and grant proposals by other researchers for the journals and funding agencies. And well known professors like Dr. Perry served on agency funding panels and traveled frequently for invited talks and site visits to evaluate departments at other universities.

And last, but by no means the least, a professor spent countless hours attending committee meetings to conduct departmental business. Here, the routine for Dr. Perry was anything but normal, as both Dr. Perry and Dr. Bates were present in many of the meetings. The tension ionized the air in the conference room. With everyone aware of the situation, no one could keep their eyes and thoughts away from the two adversaries, and progress on matters at hand was far slower than usual, which is to say that next to nothing was accomplished during those weeks.

In mid-month, the prosecutor asked for a pre-trial conference with Paul and his attorneys. They met on the afternoon of Thursday, July 15, in a conference room in the office wing of the courthouse.

The prosecutor leaned his elbows on the table, made a tent with his fingers, narrowed his eyes and regarded Paul with a smarmy, patronizing smile. "Mr. Tyson, we would like to offer you a deal."

Craig Basham and Hal Holmes had presumed correctly that this was the purpose of the meeting and had discussed the likely scenarios with Paul on the previous day.

"What might that be?" Paul asked the prosecutor.

"We would be willing to reduce the charge from first degree murder to second degree murder, in return for a guilty plea."

"Why would I want to do that?"

"Surely you know that this would reduce the sentence from mandatory life down to life or any number of years. We would not ask for life. Your chances of getting out way before old age would be very good. Virtually certain, I would think."

Paul would have none of it. He was not going to plead guilty no matter what they offered. "Not a chance, Mr. prosecutor. Not a chance in hell. The only deal I would entertain would be having the charge dismissed and this damn ankle collar taken off immediately, in return for an expression of my undying thanks."

"We'll see how you feel about it on August second, when the judge starts to seat a jury. Things will start to come into pretty sharp focus about that time, Mr. Tyson. And you might want to rethink the caliber of legal advice you're getting, son."

The prosecutor stood and nodded to Paul's attorneys. They glared back at the prosecutor and watched him leave the room.

"I wonder if this signals that he's not so confident about his case, or just the normal fear of unpredictable juries and wanting a sure thing," said Craig.

"We'll never know," said Hal. "Shall we adjourn to the nearest brew pub?"

"Indeed," said Craig.

Also in mid-month, Paul's father, Brian Tyson, called Paul from Europe to express his support. He volunteered to pay Paul's legal expenses, but Paul said that was not necessary. Tyson senior also said that he would be able to return stateside by the end of the month and would attend the trial. They hadn't been together since Christmas, and Paul hated for this to be the scene of their reunion, but he looked forward to seeing his old man. His dad had not missed a single one of Paul's football games, and it was nice to know he wouldn't be missing this battle either.

By the end of July, everyone in Paul's camp was as ready as they could be for the trial. Let's get on with it, they all felt. On Friday, July 30, Paul, Craig Basham and Hal Holmes met for a final discussion of their defense strategy. From the list of witnesses the prosecution would be calling, they planned the questions they would ask in cross examination. They settled on the sequence of defense witnesses they would call. They still had nothing with which to blow the prosecution's case right out of the water; the overall goal remained convincing the jury that there was reasonable doubt that Paul was guilty.

# Chapter 30

During the first morning of the trial on August 2, Paul had been lost in reverie all through the questioning of five more prospective jurors, all of whom were found to be acceptable to both the defense and the prosecution. These included two more housewives, a motel manager, a crane operator and a high school coach.

Paul's attention returned to the courtroom when the judge ordered an hour break for lunch. The remaining uncalled prospective jurors in the gallery were directed to return to the jury pool room downstairs where there was an adjacent cafeteria, and the bailiff led the fourteen people in the jury box through the rear door of the courtroom and down the hall to the jury room where box lunches would be brought to them. Everyone else left for nearby restaurants.

The court was reconvened at one p.m. Seated in the sparse audience behind Paul were Joan, Dr. Perry, and his father Brian. Also seated there were institute director Dr. Tollefson and marine superintendent Dave Washington. Ron Withers' family was in their usual place behind the prosecutor's table.

The bailiff called prospective juror number four to the stand. James Stimson was a marina service manager. He knew very little about the case, knew no one at RULI and no one in law enforcement. Craig Basham and Hal Holmes thought Stimson would understand the danger of the self-closing hatch and the likelihood of an accidental injury, and hoped he would get past the prosecutor. No such luck. The prosecutor saw the same possibility, and wanting no part of it, used a second peremptory challenge. "I thank and excuse Mr. Stimson." He was replaced by another prospective juror.

Two more prospectives passed muster: number two, waitress Carmen Baker, and number eighteen, general contractor Henry Cunningham. Neither knew about the case and had no confounding connections.

Jennifer Stone, number eight, was a real estate agent. Craig asked if she knew about the case.

"I read something about it, and my son talked about it."

"How does your son know about it?"

"He is a junior at the university, and apparently it is generally known on campus."

"Can you be objective as a juror in this case?"

"I think so."

Craig conferred with Hal Holmes. Then he addressed the judge. "Your honor, defense wishes to challenge for cause."

The judge asked Ms. Stone, "Does your son have any opinion about the case?"

"I don't think so."

After some thought, the judge decided to deny the challenge for cause.

Craig and Hal conferred again. They were still concerned that, as a mother of an undergrad at the university, she might tend to be sympathetic to Withers and his family. They decided to use a peremptory. Craig said, "I thank and excuse Ms. Stone."

The prospective jury pool was dwindling. But when Number 24 was called to the stand, bank teller Earl Connors turned out to be acceptable to both the prosecution and the defense. This finally completed the jury with twelve active members and two alternate members. It was now two-thirty.

The prosecutor liked to start fresh in the morning with his case, and he asked the judge for an adjournment until morning. The judge was reluctant to waste time, but he did have plenty of other matters back in his chambers, so he agreed. The fourteen jurors were instructed not to discuss the case, read about it, or watch TV coverage of it. They were instructed to report to the jury room at eight-thirty in the morning. Court would come to order at nine a.m.

Paul joined Crag and Hal at Craig's office for coffee. They all agreed that the jury looked reasonable with no one showing any obvious biases, although one never knew for sure about those things. Later Paul had dinner with his dad and Joan, and they strolled around Clinch Park on the bay for a while. Joan dropped off Paul and his dad at *Tondeleyo*.

"Good luck tomorrow. We'll be cheering in the peanut gallery."

"Thanks Joan. See you there."

## Chapter 31

Tuesday morning at nine a.m. the court reconvened. The prosecutor began his opening statement. With cloying drama, he said that he and his witnesses would show beyond a reasonable doubt that Paul Tyson murderously and fatally assaulted Ronald Withers in the storeroom in the aft of the research vessel *Halcyon* on the morning of Saturday, June 12. Sneering toward Paul, the prosecutor said that he would provide convincing evidence of Tyson's motive and opportunity, and would show the connection of both the defendant and the victim to the murder weapon, the heavy hatch door that Tyson had so viciously thrown down on Ronald Withers.

With calm confidence, Craig hoisted his big frame to its full six-one, briefly regarded the prosecutor with a level stare, and turned to the jury with an All-America smile. He quietly but firmly stated that he would convince them that the prosecution's case against Paul Tyson was entirely circumstantial, and that the evidence for a tragically accidental injury was extremely strong. In summary, he said he fully expected that the jury would have great and reasonable doubt of any guilt on the part of this honorable young man.

The prosecutor called the first of his witnesses who would establish the occurrence of Paul's angry threat at the scientific conference in Ann Arbor. He began with Dr. Bates, who had been right in front of Ron Withers in the cafeteria line.

"Dr. Bates, what did Paul Tyson do and say in the cafeteria of the conference center in Ann Arbor on June seventh?"

"Paul slammed Ron against the wall and said he would break his neck."

"Break his neck if what?"

"If Ron wouldn't retract our journal article."

"Retract it for what reason?"

Bates drew a breath for a beat. "Because he thought Ron had used some of his research data," he said in a small voice with downcast eyes.

"No further questions, your honor," said the prosecutor.

Craig Basham rose to cross examine. "Dr. Bates, isn't the phrase 'or I'll break your neck' a common, empty threat that lots of people make in the heat of an argument, but don't mean literally?"

"Objection," blurted the prosecutor.

"Sustained," said the judge. "You need not answer that, Dr. Bates."

"No further questions," said Craig.

The prosecutor started to call his next witness of Paul's threat. Craig interrupted him, wanting to prevent the damage of a parade of repeated references to the threat.

"Your honor, defense will stipulate the occurrence of the threat by the defendant. We would prefer to move along in the case."

The judge agreed to that, and instructed the prosecutor to proceed.

The prosecutor called a couple of students who had seen Paul's anger and heard him throw his sea bag down in the forecastle on the morning of *Halcyon's* cruise. Craig had no questions. He didn't want to dwell on this emphasis on Paul's anger at Withers. And he would wait until his closing statement to point out that educated professionals can be angry about plagiarism without resorting to assault; indeed there have been countless incidents of scientific plagiarism but no related cases of assault that he knew of.

The prosecutor then called a forensic technician, who showed enlarged photos of the injured Ron Withers in the hold, and of the hatch. The technician cited the DNA evidence of Withers' hair on the underside of the hatch, and the fingerprints of Paul Tyson on the handle of hatch. Ron Withers' mother whimpered behind the railing like an abandoned kitten.

Craig rose to cross examine the tech regarding the fingerprints. "Did you find any other person's prints on that hatch handle?"

"Yes."

"Would you say several people?"

"Yes"

"Would you say the prints of most of the scientific personnel of the institute were on that handle?"

"Objection," called the prosecutor.

The judge overruled and allowed the witness to answer.

"There were many other prints, but we were looking for Mr. Tyson's."

Craig continued, "Wouldn't it be normal and expected to find Mr. Tyson's prints among those of all the RULI personnel who frequent that equipment hold?"

"I wouldn't know about that," replied the tech.

"Thank you," said Craig. "No further questions."

The prosecutor called Larry Griffin to the stand. "Mr. Griffin, were you aboard the ship the morning Mr. Withers was attacked?"

"Objection," said Craig. "The question presumes the event of an attack."

"Sustained. Rephrase."

"Mr. Griffin, were you aboard the ship the morning Mr. Withers was fatally injured?"

"Yes."

Were you aware of Paul Tyson's whereabouts that morning?"

"Yes."

"How so?"

"I was in Dr. Bates' cabin with a view of the boat deck where Tyson was sitting."

"Did Mr. Tyson leave that location during the morning?"

"Yes, he went below about the time we rounded Lighthouse Point."

The prosecutor then produced an affidavit from the marine inspector that stated that the last time anyone saw Ron Withers was shortly before the ship rounded the point.

Craig rose to question Griffin. "Mr. Griffin you did not come forward with this testimony until at least three weeks after the incident. Why is that?"

"Paul is a good friend of mine, and I had a hard time bringing myself to do this."

Paul rolled his eyes, and Joan closed hers and shook her head.

"Isn't it a fact that you came forward with this unfavorable testimony after an unsuccessful attempt to seduce Paul's friend Joan Brockton?"

"Objection!" barked the prosecutor

"Sustained," replied the judge. "That was right out of left field, counselor."

"Your honor," replied Craig, "we will establish the relevance of that question during our defense. No further questions."

"Mr. Prosecutor?" said the judge.

"I have no further witnesses, your honor."

The Judge declared a lunch break; court was to reconvene at two p.m. The courtroom emptied quickly. On the way out, Hal Holmes said to Craig, "Prosecutor's throwing hardballs, but you're getting a piece of some of them. Let's keep sowing the seeds of doubt wherever we can."

# Chapter 32

At two p.m., the first witness for the defense was sworn in, and Craig Basham addressed him.

"Captain Robado, would you please explain what we are about to see in the video clip?" A computer, digital projector, and screen had been set up in view of all in the courtroom.

Robado began. "This is the hatch cover that hit Ron Withers. The video sequence shows that it easily slammed over by itself when the ship was rocking in the trough of large waves. It was because when open, it was held at an angle by that chain, but it was not restrained from behind. The chain has since been removed, but it was there on June twelfth."

An assistant of Craig's ran the clip several times. Craig asked, "Captain, what is the possibility of the hatch severely injuring someone in that hold by closing in that way?"

"Just before we shot that clip, a student was nearly hit in the head that way. If she had straightened up in that shallow hold two seconds earlier, she would have been injured the same way Mr. Withers was."

"The hatch is that heavy, and closes that fast by itself?"

"Absolutely."

"Was the sea as rough on the morning of June twelfth as it was when this video was shot?"

"It was rougher," replied Robado.

"Captain, would you please explain to the jury what 'in the trough' means?"

"It means the ship is sideways to the waves, producing the most violent rolling."

"Was the ship ever in the trough on the morning of June twelfth?"

"We were in the trough for about ten minutes, before rounding the Leelanau peninsula."

"How does that correlate to the time Mr. Withers became missing?"

"According to all accounts, Mr. Withers was last seen shortly before the ship left the lee of the peninsula."

"Captain, I have a different question now. In your inquiries of ship's personnel after the incident on June twelfth, did anyone tell you that they had seen Paul Tyson go below while you were underway that morning?"

"No."

"Specifically, did Larry Griffin tell you that?"

"No."

"Thank you. No further questions at this time."

The prosecutor rose and asked Captain Robado if he could verify that the video was authentic. Robado glared at him, but before he could answer, Craig interceded.

"Your honor, my next witness will speak to that."

As the prosecutor had no other questions, the Judge allowed Craig to call the county marine inspector to the witness box.

"Sir, you have seen the video. Can you verify its authenticity?"

"Yes. My staff and I have been given a demonstration of this phenomenon. We were taken out on the ship on a rough day, and with the ship in the trough, the hatch behaved that way several times."

"During your demonstration, was the sea similarly rough as it was on the morning of June twelfth?"

"It was probably rougher on June twelfth," replied the inspector. "That was a major windstorm."

"Inspector, in your inquiries of ship's personnel after the incident on June twelfth, was their testimony consistent with the facts as just now related by Captain Robado?"

"Yes"

"Did anyone tell you that they had seen Paul Tyson go below while you were underway that morning?"

"No."

"Specifically, did Larry Griffin tell you that?"

"No."

"Thank you. No further questions at this time."

The prosecutor did not cross examine the inspector.

Craig then called his third witness. Looking as though she was about to walk barefoot into a room full of scorpions, Joan approached the witness box and was sworn in.

"Ms. Brockton, on the night of Saturday, June nineteenth, you went to dinner and dancing with Mr. Larry Griffin, is that correct?"

Joan shuddered. "Yes, I did."

"What happened after leaving the dancing establishment?"

"Larry drove me to my apartment. I had had way too much to drink, and I stupidly let him come in." It was killing Joan to say this. "Larry became amorous, so to speak. When I didn't cooperate, he told me he knew Dr. Bates had been in his cabin all that morning and knew that Paul had not left the deck. Larry said he would help out with Paul's case if I would sleep with him. When I refused, he got angry and threatened to testify against Paul. He said he would claim to have seen Paul go below." Joan dabbed at a tear.

Several jurors squirmed in their chairs and looked at each other.

"Thank you Ms. Brockton. That's all."

The prosecutor rose, and slowly stalked toward Joan like a jungle cat approaching a small goat tied to a stake. He actually licked his chops.

"Ms. Brockton. Can you name anyone who saw you with Mr. Griffin anywhere that night?"

"No."

"Was anyone else in your apartment that night?"

"No."

"Is there any independent corroboration of your testimony whatsoever?"

"No"

"Now let me ask you this. Paul Tyson is your lover, isn't that correct?"

Joan skipped a beat. "Paul is my friend."

"How much of a friend?"

"He is a very good friend."

"I could probably find people who could testify that you are romantically involved with Mr. Tyson, couldn't I?"

"I suppose so."

"Yes or no, Ms. Brockton."

"Yes."

"So you have a major vested interest in helping Mr. Tyson's defense, don't you?"

"I would help anyone who I knew was wrongly accused, as Paul is."

"And can you provide verifiable direct evidence to refute the charge against Mr. Tyson?"

"No."

The prosecutor turned to the jury, paused dramatically, and said, "I have no need for further questions of this witness."

Craig took a deep breath and stood up. "Your honor, I have only one more witness, but much to cover. It is getting a little late in the day, and I suspect that everyone would prefer to start fresh in the morning. May I respectfully request an adjournment until tomorrow?"

The judge asked the prosecutor if he objected. The prosecutor, flush from his mauling of Joan's testimony, was way ahead on points. He did not object at all to an early cocktail hour.

"Very well," said the Judge. He gave the jury the standard instructions about not discussing the case with anyone overnight, and then adjourned the court until nine the next morning.

As everyone rose to leave, Craig asked Paul to meet with him and Harold Holmes at Craig's house after dinner to discuss the game plan for tomorrow. Paul nodded and moved away to join his dad and Joan. As Craig and Harold were putting their note pads in their briefcases, they agreed with each other that, although the prosecution's case was still circumstantial, the prosecutor was doing well, and Griffin's testimony was especially damaging.

Harold said, "We don't have much choice but to get Paul up there tomorrow and try to make him look good, and then sow some big seeds of doubt in the jury during closing argument." Craig nodded.

# Chapter 33

Paul, his dad and Joan went from the courthouse over to a brew pub on Front Street for a beer or two before dinner. At shortly after four p.m., it was not yet crowded, and they could talk quietly over their mugs of refreshing draft. As they chatted, Brian Tyson wondered aloud how common plagiarism was in the professional scientific literature. Paul said he thought that it was more common than most people realize, but there was no way to know for sure.

"But most don't get away with it, at least in cases where the research is important and noteworthy," said Paul. "In those cases, the work gets scrutinized closely, and other workers try to replicate it or incorporate it in further study, and the fraud shows up. That gets reported fairly regularly in journals like *Science*. Obscure stuff of low importance may go unnoticed, but in that case the plagiarist doesn't make much career progress anyway."

Then Joan said, "Unfortunately some of the kids are getting an early start. Last week, one of my Bio 101 students turned in a paper that was way too well-written for the normal freshman. Last night I decided to type some of his lines into Google to see what would happen. In two seconds, up popped a published article with passages identical to those in his report. The more I typed, the more I found. Nailed his ass."

Paul was staring at Joan with his mouth open. He set his beer mug down hard on the table top, sloshing out some of it.

"My god. Where has my blind-ass brain been? Why haven't I thought of trying that. We've got to get over to the lab. I've got to get online."

Paul slapped a twenty onto the table and started for the door. His dad and Joan looked at each other, and hurried after him. The Mustang flew the few blocks to the institute like it was at the Sunday drag races. Paul didn't notice that the steering was getting a little loose.

At the computer, Paul queried Google Scholar for articles by Dr. Bates, including two coauthored with Ron Withers. Then he cut and pasted some passages from them back into Google. Bates' papers came back up, of course, but so did some by other authors with identical passages, all with earlier publication dates. When Paul was finished, he had six of Bates' articles and ten by other authors that Bates had clearly plagiarized.

"Got the bastard," Paul said. "These are all pretty obscure journals he used, mostly foreign. But he is guilty as hell of scientific misconduct. Christ, all this time I've been focusing on Withers. I almost missed this."

He made a Xerox copy of the whole stack, and called Craig Basham. "Got to see you immediately. Can you get Holmes over there right now? Well, try then. I'll be there in five minutes." His dad and Joan hurried after him again.

"Drive slower for Christ sake, Paul," Joan pleaded.

Paul did no such thing. He drove the final block at forty mph and braked hard as he turned left into Craig's driveway. The right front wheel hit the curb, the tie rod snapped, and Paul lost control. The car glanced off the big sycamore tree and spun around backwards across the sidewalk into the front yard.

"Good god," cried Brian Tyson. "Everyone okay?"

Everyone was shaken, but none was hurt. They slowly got out of the car. Craig Basham rushed out of the house into the yard.

"I think those bastards fucked with my car," said Paul, still breathing hard.

"What bastards?" asked Paul's dad.

"Same ones who tried to sink my boat," said Paul.

Paul went around to the left front wheel, dropped to the ground and slid under the bumper on his back.

"Yep. The left tie rod is hacksawed most of the way through, like I'm sure the right one was. We're damn lucky we weren't on the highway when it let go. That's probably what they had in mind."

Brian Tyson watched his son get back up off the ground. "You've got to do something about those guys, Paul."

Craig Basham explained that there was not much they could do legally at this point, and gave a strong warning against any vigilante action that would add to Paul's problems.

"But they are going to make a mistake sooner or later that we can make use of," continued Craig. "They already showed they can do that when they underestimated Paul in the drunk tank. Let's go in and call a wrecker to get this thing out of here, and then show me what the hell brought you here in such a hurry."

In his living room, Craig looked through the Xeroxed material as they waited for Harold to arrive. Finally Hal came to the door. "Wife's not pleased. What's the deal?"

Craig explained the stack of paper, and Hal whistled at the ceiling.

"You've got to lay this on Bates tomorrow morning," said Paul.

Craig demurred. "Paul, this is going to dig your hole deeper, in terms of the motive aspect of their case." Craig looked at Hal with questioning eyebrows.

"Craig, I have to agree with Paul. Bates is the key to all this. Right now things are way up in the air, with the prosecution ahead on points. And we all know what a crapshoot juries are. You just never know. We need to shake Bates loose somehow. This may do it."

"I agree," said Paul.

"Okay," said Craig. "We'll run with it. But we need a Plan B for tomorrow, in case Bates doesn't fall apart. Joan, would you order us all some takeout?"

They got busy. Interrupted only by the arrival of the wrecker truck, they finally finished up at nine p.m. Craig drove Paul and his dad back to Paul's boat at RULI, and dropped Joan off at her apartment.

Later that night, Paul lay sleepless in his bunk. His mind would not stop running the continually looping scenes of the last many weeks since he first saw the Withers and Bates paper in the journal. *Couldn't I have just quietly told Ron I knew what he did? Couldn't I have been civil to Joan so she wouldn't have gotten tangled up with Griffin?* Drenched in sweat, he realized just how close he was to going to prison. He knew Basham and Holmes were doing all they could, but he also knew that they did not have a whole lot of control over this thing.

At two a.m. Paul got up, dressed, and quietly left the boat. He walked around the docks for over an hour. Finally he pulled out his cell phone and called Joan.

"I can't sleep either," she said. "Come on over."

Paul walked the few blocks to Joan's apartment. She made some hot chocolate, and they watched an old movie on cable from her narrow bed until finally drifting off to sleep for a couple of hours.

# Chapter

## 34

Wednesday morning at nine a.m., the murder trial of Paul Tyson reconvened in the courtroom. The prosecutor looked fresh and confident. The two defense attorneys whispered a few words to each other, and Craig Basham rose from his seat.

"The defense recalls Dr. Eldon Bates."

The prosecutor was caught completely off guard and started massaging the back of his ear as though he thought he wasn't hearing right this morning. Dr. Bates seemed just as startled, and he slowly took the stand with a quizzical furrow on his brow. The court reminded Bates that he was still under oath from yesterday. He nodded absently.

"Dr. Bates, where were you during the morning of the events on the *Halcyon* on the morning of June twelfth?"

"I was in my cabin, the chief scientist's cabin aft of the bridge, the whole morning."

"Doing what, Dr. Bates?"

"Working at my computer on a grant proposal."

"Yesterday Larry Griffin testified that you could see Paul Tyson from where you were sitting. Is that correct?"

"Yes, I was facing my aft window with a view of the port side of the lifeboat deck."

"Did he leave at any time?"

"I don't know." Bates was looking down now.

"Was Paul Tyson's accusation of plagiarism by Ronald Withers accurate, regarding the data in your journal article with him?"

"I don't know." Bates was still looking down, blinking rapidly.

"Have you ever engaged in plagiarism, Dr. Bates?"

Bates reddened as the prosecutor exploded off his chair and shouted his objection.

"Sustained," said the Judge. "Be careful, Mr. Basham."

Craig paused, and then said, "Permission to approach the witness, your honor?"

"You may."

Indeed, Craig had to be very careful now. He casually picked up the stack of copies of Bates' publications and the plagiarized material, and walked quickly to the witness stand. "Dr. Bates, I want you to look at these papers for a moment."

Bates rose apprehensively, but his hand reflexively accepted the stack of papers. He took one brief look, knowing immediately what this was, and his chin fell to his chest as the prosecutor rose to object again.

"Your honor, whatever that is, it has not been entered here properly, and..."

The prosecutor's words were eclipsed as Dr. Bates let go of the paper stack, and it bounced off of the railing of the witness box and out onto the floor, pages sliding and splaying out everywhere, some of them all the way out to the railing in front of the spectators. The jury all gasped as one. Their eyes returned to Dr. Bates, who now gripped the railing with white knuckles and trembled like a wet kid in a chilly wind on a beach.

After a moment, the judge broke the stunned silence. "Mr. Basham, you have not properly..."

"WAIT. Wait," blurted Dr. Bates. "Your honor," he continued in a halting, cracking voice, "I can't let this go on any longer. I ... I've been lying ever since the morning poor

Ron got hurt. I did see Paul the whole time, and he was sitting or lying there beside the lifeboat the entire time. To leave, he would have had to pass right in front of my window. He did not do that.

Bates took a deep breath. He had control of his voice now. "The simple truth is that Ron's injury was a tragic accident. By allowing Paul to get convicted and discredited, I was hoping to protect my shameful secret. But Paul is guilty of exactly nothing here, and did not deserve my treachery in the least; and it would only have been a matter of time for my career to implode in any case."

Bates took another deep breath. "The sad thing is, Ron was probably in the process of hiding or retrieving the data books he stole from Paul. He was trying to help me in my despicable publishing charade, the charade that has been unmasked here on the floor before you. I was leading that poor young man down my dark path, and he paid for it with his life."

Another deep breath. Dr. Bates was still not finished. He was breaking down now, and it was coming out in gulping, barking sobs. "The worst of it, your honor, the very worst of it is this: it was I who rigged that goddamned chain on the hatch cover. I did that just the day before the cruise. Can you imagine? Too lazy to lift the heavy hatch cover off the deck to close it every time, and not seaman enough to realize the danger of the stupid chain rig.

"So I literally set the trap that accidentally killed poor Ron. And thereby endangered the careers of three fine professionals at the institute – Tony Robado, Dave Washington, and Karen Tollefson – by exposing them to this colossal liability situation."

A final pause. "So I am the guilty one here. *I* am the guilty one."

Sitting now with his head cradled in the palm of his left hand, Dr. Bates was finally finished. His eyes were focused on the hundred or so pages of deceit that lay all over the floor before him, the remains of a career that had ruptured and scattered into useless tatters to be shredded and discarded in a landfill of despair.

Silence descended over the courtroom like a quilted shroud. Paul stared at Dr. Bates, gradually assimilating all that he had just heard. In the audience, Joan was awash in tears, her trembling hands clasped in her lap.

Craig Basham broke the silence. "Your honor, in the light of the testimony we have just heard, I respectfully ask that the charge against Paul Tyson be dismissed."

The judge asked Craig and the prosecutor to approach the bench. After a few words with them, he announced, "The charge against Paul Tyson is hereby dismissed. This court is adjourned."

In the ensuing bustle of people rising and moving around, the judge called Craig back over to him. "That was very risky, Basham. If the professor hadn't broken your way, I would have thrown you and that undeclared stack of paper out of here. I'm still within an inch of citing you for contempt of court. Now go enjoy your victory." Craig nodded, but he couldn't stifle his growing smile. He returned beaming to Paul.

"You may have to bail *me* out now, Paul. But it was worth it."

After shaking hands with Craig, Harold, and Dr. Perry, Paul turned to Joan. She locked her arms around him and nearly broke one of his ribs. After a moment, they walked over to the Withers family. Mrs. Withers was crumpled in her chair. Mr. Withers rose and slowly extended his hand to Paul, who then said, "Mr. Withers, I never wanted Ron hurt. I just..."

The man put his hand on Paul's shoulder and nodded. "I understand, son."

Paul turned to his own father, who was talking with Craig Basham. Father and son embraced fiercely.

"Well, Dad, you can get back to work across the pond over there, building more empires."

"Not so fast, Fireball. I came all this way, I intend to get in some sailing on that fancy 'yatch' of yours." He had always called yachts *yatches*, mocking the upper crust in his frugal early years.

"Not a bad idea," said Paul. "How about getting started with that today? How about all of you? Got time for a good sail? Hal, are your kids available for their first lesson?"

"I think so," said Holmes, getting out his cell phone.

Everyone else agreed readily, except for RULI director Karen Tollefson. This was no time for her to be celebrating. Despite Paul's exoneration, she still carried the weight of the liability issue that loomed over the institute.

Paul started toward the doors, when the prosecutor stepped in front of Paul. "You got something of ours." Paul shot back a scowl, and then realized immediately what the man was talking about. The bailiff produced a key to unlock the ankle collar.

"Watch that short fuse sonny. It'll get you sooner or later," the prosecutor said.

Paul contemplated saying something like *Hey you jerk, I've got my anger under control now, so fuck off.* But he figured the prosecutor would fail to see the ironic humor in that, so he said nothing. The prosecutor turned on his heel and walked away.

Paul continued up the aisle toward the doors, followed by his retinue. Outside they all agreed to meet at the RULI parking lot at one-thirty that afternoon, after Paul got his bail money back and they all had lunch.

# Chapter

## *35*

*Tondeleyo* was close-hauled in a twelve knot northeast wind, heeling to port as she boiled along northward up the West Arm of Traverse Bay toward Bowers Harbor, partway up Old Mission Peninsula. Eight people were comfortably distributed around her cockpit and deck. Harold Holmes' two kids were already engaged in their sailing lesson, trimming sheets and steering and feeling enormously important there among all those grownups.

Behind the boy at the wheel, Paul stood in the bright sunshine with his back against the mizzen mast, looking along the length of his command with the pleasant calm of a man whose life had just been handed back to him. Joan was at his side. Craig, Harold, and Dr. Perry chatted back and forth across the cockpit, and Brian Tyson made numerous trips below to his stash of beer he had brought for everyone in a Styrofoam cooler of ice. But Paul stuck to his no-drinking rule for himself as captain while underway.

After passing out another round of Landshark, Brian Tyson asked Craig, "What would you have done if Dr. Bates hadn't cracked this morning?"

"First, I would have tried to get the plagiarism papers properly admitted as a defense exhibit, in order to discredit Dr. Bates and throw doubt on his testimony. The judge gave me holy hell for the stunt, but he probably would have admitted the stuff eventually. After all, plagiarism was at the heart of the matter. In any case, I would have called Joan to explain how we obtained the material, and I would have called RULI Director Dr. Tollefson to the stand to explain how plagiarism is one of the forms of scientific misconduct that forever destroys the credibility of a scientist.

"Then in my closing statement, I would have emphasized the circumstantial evidence and the fact that no one saw Paul assault Withers. I would have emphasized how easily the accident could have happened, indeed did happen. I would have stated that there is no history that I could find of violence associated with academic plagiarism, and even during the decades of the most vicious scientific feuding ever in America, between paleontologists Charles Marsh and Edward Cope in the nineteenth century, countless priceless fossils were stolen or destroyed and vast sums of research funding were lost but nobody was assaulted or murdered.

"And finally I would have said that the testimony of Dr. Bates and Larry Griffin was self-serving and lacked credibility, and that doubt about Paul's alleged involvement was not only reasonable but overwhelming. And I would have hoped for the best. But if Bates hadn't cracked, I think our chances of winning were not real good." That got everyone silent for a while.

Having sailed past the west side of Marion Island, Paul had the kids tack the boat around so that *Tondeleyo* could beat up into Bowers Harbor.

"Sally, get the starboard jib sheet ready on the winch head. Now go over to the port sheet and stand by for my 'helm's alee' command. When I give it, release the sheet and go back to the starboard winch and start winding that sheet in as fast as you can. Ready? Okay.

"Now Joey, start steering around to starboard; that's right. When I call 'meet her', steer back straight ahead.

"Okay Sally, HELM'S ALEE. That's good, just drop that sheet on the deck. Now get over and wind the starbord winch fast. Both hands. Very good."

The big jenny clattered and roared as it luffed its way around the main mast, and then it stiffened up on the starbord tack. The main and mizzen booms flopped over by themselves.

"Okay, meet her, Joey. Stay on this heading. Perfect. Sally, tighten the main and mizzen sheets a little. Perfect. What a team!"

Hal Holmes grinned at his kids with both thumbs up.

Just after six p.m. they rounded up into Bowers Harbor along the west side of Old Mission Peninsula. Anchoring at the head of the harbor, Paul ferried the group in the dinghy, two at a time, over to the dock adjacent to the restaurant. The wives of Dr. Perry, Craig Basham, and Hal Holmes had all driven up from Traverse City to meet the sailing party at the restaurant.

The large group was seated at two tables pushed together for the occasion. The early evening sun blazed through the big bay windows and burnished the shiny maple furniture. A pretty good local wine was served all around, and juice for the kids.

Dr. Perry led off with a toast to Paul. "To our guest of honor. Welcome back to the free world, Paul."

Paul followed with a toast to Craig Basham and Hal Holmes. "To my crack legal staff. My undying thanks, gentlemen."

Then Paul said, "Wait a minute, I've forgotten something." Everyone pondered this as Paul got out his cell phone.

"Martin, you old sea dog. Yeah, it's me. Got good news. Case is over. I'm a free man. Yes, everyone is very happy. Look, thanks a million again for helping with the boat. I owe you big time. Oh yes I do, Marty. Okay, take care my friend."

Delicious meals were ordered and consumed, with quiet banter around the table. Most of them had the signature

Great Lakes dish, broiled whitefish, sweet and succulent. Paul turned to the two kids. "Are you guys ready for sailing lessons every week?" They both nodded enthusiastically. "Next time, Sally steers and Joey mans the sheets." Sally grinned widely.

At seven-thirty, Perry, Craig, and Hal and his kids said their goodbyes and left with their wives for the drive home. Paul, his dad, and Joan returned to *Tondeleyo* for the sail back to the RULI harbor.

As they sailed slowly southward in a falling wind, Paul's father got to talking about the idea of a circumnavigation of Lake Michigan in *Tondeleyo*, with a few days' stopover in Chicago to see numerous old friends. Paul thought this was a great idea.

"Joan?"

"Paul, I'd love to do that, but I have to teach. No way I could get away during the next few weeks. Anyway, that trip should be just the two of you."

Paul nodded. She was right, as usual.

They sat in silence for a while and then performed a controlled jibe as the wind shifted to the northwest. They continued in silence for the final run down into the RULI harbor, *Tondeleyo's* wake chuckling along behind them.

# CHAPTER 36

Two days later, Paul and Joan drove Brian Tyson to the airport. Paul's dad needed to get back to his business operations in Europe; he would need to change planes in Detroit for the 7:30 p.m. flight to Amsterdam. Nearing the security station, the two men faced each other.

"Let's work on that plan to cruise around Lake Michigan, Paul. I'll be back from Europe in a couple of weeks."

"You got it, Dad. Thanks for being here. Have a good trip."

Brian Tyson embraced Paul and then Joan, and he got in line. Paul and Joan walked back out to Joan's Blazer.

They drove in the pleasant late afternoon sun back into town for a couple of brews and an early dinner. They chatted idly, still getting used to life without the pall of the looming trial they had endured for weeks.

Comfortably fed, Paul and Joan strolled out into the pub's parking lot. As they approached her Blazer, a familiar rumble turned their heads. They recognized Jake's white truck entering the lot and reached quickly for Joan's car doors. But Jake pulled his truck behind the Blazer and blocked it in. The F150 bucked and shook as the engine idled roughly. Jake and Arty both stared at Paul with the bleary red eyes of a day-long drinking binge.

"You guys out sawing more tie rods today?" said Paul.

Jake squinted, obviously struggling to understand the question. Then he slowly grinned. He tried to spit tobacco juice out his window, but only managed to dribble it down his chin and onto his tee shirt. The shirt looked like it had been though this many times.

"Wh- wh- where's that fancy Mustang, Tyson?" Jake giggled, then laughed himself into a racking cough. He winced and held his ribs, still sore from the drunk tank fight.

"You know damn well, shit brain," said Paul.

"Paul, be careful," Joan warned.

"Well, have a nice day, lovebirds," said Jake with another racking cough. He pulled the truck around the lot and out onto the street, rumbling and smoking like it was burning old tires for fuel.

Paul and Joan waited a bit, and then drove out of the lot toward the institute. They did not notice Jake and Arty watch them drive by from a side street and then pull out to follow from a distance. When Paul and Joan reached the institute, Jake parked where he could see across U.S. 31; the institute parking lot, harbor and docks were in full view. He shut off the engine, cracked open two more beers, and waited.

Paul and Joan parked and walked out onto the main dock to watch the gathering sunset. The sun was still well above the horizon, but pink and orange were beginning to show behind the low streaky clouds. Stopping alongside the *Halcyon*, Paul gazed up at his "station" at the lifeboat, remembering the last time he had been up there.

"I'm allowed aboard her now, aren't I?"

"Yes you are," said Joan. "Want to?"

"No, not right now."

As they turned back to look across the dock at the sunset, the quiet scene was shattered by a screech and a roar from up in the parking lot. They stood dumbfounded as the white truck rocketed down through the lot and out onto the dock. Reflexes fired and Paul and Joan ran for the side of the dock. The truck swerved left toward them and bore down with Jake's eyes blazing. Diving for the water, they felt the concussive wind as the truck passed within inches of them and then smashed into a large steel mooring bollard near the edge of the dock. The fifty miles-per-hour momentum flipped the truck up and over on its back, and the cab was crushed nearly flat as the truck bounced off the edge of the dock into the water in a hail of splinters.

Paul and Joan were underwater when the truck splashed in, and when they resurfaced all they saw was bubbles foaming up about twenty feet from them.

"Are you okay, Joan?"

"Yes."

"I'm going down there."

"What?"

"I have to. They don't deserve it, but I gotta try to get them out."

"Well, let's go," said Joan.

They both dove in the thirteen feet of water and followed the trail of bubbles. There wasn't much light, but they could see the truck lying on its side. There were no more than a few inches between the crushed cab top and the window sills. The water inside the cab was turning crimson, and there was no movement in there. Paul and Joan pulled hard to open the door, but it was hopelessly jammed. With aching lungs they pushed off toward the surface and broke out gasping for air. They looked up and saw David Washington on the dock with a cell phone at his ear. Washington grabbed a life ring from its stanchion and threw it down to them.

"I saw the whole thing. I thought it hit you. Are you okay?"

"Yes," replied Paul, "but those guys aren't. There's no way. There's a lot of blood, they're not moving, and the cab is crushed so bad we can't get them out."

Washington relayed that information to the 911 operator, and spoke again to Paul and Joan.

"EMS, divers, and a crane truck are on the way. There's a ladder out at the end of the dock. Can you make it out there?"

"Yes," said both swimmers.

By the time they had swum to the ladder, climbed out and walked dripping wet back to where Dave Washington was, the rescue vehicles were roaring into the parking lot. Joan had dejá vue seeing the emergency lights flashing all over the dock again.

Divers with pry bars hit the water and dove to the wreck. The crane truck began unreeling its lift cable over the side. A police Crown Vic pulled up, and out stepped none other than Officer 23.

*This guy is everywhere*, thought Paul, shivering harder now than he already was from the cool wind on his wet clothes.

"You again, Tyson?"

Paul did not answer. Dave Washington stepped between them.

"Officer, I can explain the incident. I saw the whole thing from the office window. Let's let these two get into some dry clothes, and then they can talk to you."

The officer nodded, and then watched Paul and Joan walk around the harbor docks to *Tondeleyo*. They stepped aboard and went below, where they stripped, toweled off and dressed in some of Paul's clothes. By the time they got back to the main dock, the smashed F150 was on the dock with its doors pried open.

Jake and Arty were on their backs, and the EMS techs were pumping their chests and applying cardio shockers. But both victims obviously had massive head injuries, and vital signs were zero. Officer 23 stepped over to Paul and Joan.

"So it's your old friends, Tyson. Mr. Washington described what they did here. What a surprise. But I understand you actually tried to help them down there."

"I don't think you are surprised one bit at what they tried to do, Officer, and I think you know why my boat is here instead of Elk Rapids and why my car is in the repair shop getting a new front end."

The officer looked down at his feet and then back at Paul.

"Look Tyson, it's hard for me to admit that we were wrong about you in the Ron Withers case, but we were. I'll give you that. And you acted honorably here tonight in spite of the circumstances. I'll give you that too. But I still don't like your wise mouth, and I still don't like how you college folks think your shit don't stink. But let's do this: you keep to yourselves over here and I'll keep to myself over in town, and we'll just get along. That okay by you?"

"Okay by me," said Paul.

Paul and Joan stepped across the dock and went aboard the *Halcyon*. They leaned against the railing and watched as the two dead men were loaded into the EMS truck. The F150 was hoisted onto the crane truck, and all of the vehicles slowly backed off of the dock, turned around in the parking lot and left in a somber parade. All of the flashers were turned off. Dave Washington walked over to Paul and Joan.

"Are you guys okay?"

"Yes, Dave," replied Paul. "Listen, Joan and I will get my boat out of here tomorrow."

"There's no rush, Paul."

"Oh yes. I want *Tondeleyo* back where she belongs in Elk Rapids."

"Okay. Let me know if I can help," said Dave.

"Thanks again Dave, for your help all along in this thing."

Washington walked back to the office. Paul and Joan turned to each other, and Paul saw her tears.

"It's over, Paul."

Paul had no words. He took her hand, and they walked slowly back toward *Tondeleyo*.

# EPILOGUE

It was a calm day mid-week in late October. *Chinook*, the institute's thirty-five foot Maine lobsterman, was anchored in the mouth of the Platte River just north of Point Betsy on Lake Michigan, at the western foot of the Leelanau peninsula. With a backdrop of red- and orange-leaved maple, beech, and birch trees nestled along the shore among the evergreens, and the yellow bluffs of the Sleeping Bear dunes stretching to the north, the boat sat motionless in the early afternoon sun.

Bringing the boat around from Traverse City, Joan and Paul had stopped in at the commercial fishing docks at Leland to pick up some smoked chubs for lunch, and had enjoyed them here at anchor while watching the long V-shaped flocks of Canada geese honking and winging southward high in the sky.

In the flat calm, the only sound now was the clicking and whirring of two sport fishing reels. Paul and Joan were both seated in the stern, casting for Coho salmon returning to the river for their spawning runs. It looked like a fall vacation lark, but this was part of Joan's doctoral research. She was collecting the Coho to obtain kidney tissue in her study of the genetics of osmoregulation, or salt balance. Coho were originally ocean fish that only inhabited freshwater in coastal rivers for spawning and early development. The Great Lakes Coho had been imported here as a sport fishery, and they thrived in spite of never living in salt water.

Joan was asking what genetic mechanism turned off the normal major switch from freshwater to saltwater osmoregulation. She had three candidate regulatory genes in mind, and was working on making knockouts of them to test their physiological roles in the osmoregulation. While waiting for strikes, Joan and Paul had time for idle chatting.

"You know, I still shudder to think how close to disaster the institute came," said Joan.

"So do I," replied Paul. "We're lucky the Withers family chose to take the high road and settle for an amount that was within the university's insurance coverage. Best of all, Robado, Washington, and Tollefson all kept their jobs. I can't imagine the place without them."

"So *Halcyon* is once again a peaceful ship."

"Except when Tiny's galley gets trashed in the trough. Guy needs to get a grip."

"Don't hold your breath," said Joan. "By the way, *Halcyon* used to be a minesweeper, right? Why was the military still building wooden ships in the twentieth century?"

"They were for sweeping and detonating magnetic mines. Compared to those with steel hulls, wooden ships have a very low magnetic signature and they passed over the mines unscathed, while the high signature steel cables they towed detonated the mines safely behind them."

"You men and your wars."

"Now, now. Lots of women are warriors."

"Sadly so. Hey, speaking of my own little skirmish, I just learned that Larry Griffin is history at RULI."

"Oh really. How so?"

"While his perjury case was pending, he got nailed last month for sexual harassment of a couple of girls in the intro bio lab he was teaching. Bastard's out of the university."

"As I predicted," said Paul. "Speaking of perjury, Dr. Bates is working off his perjury sentence doing public service. I guess he also managed to get some part time teaching at a small prep school. But big-time science is definitely over for him. He did submit a retraction of the paper containing my data, so Dr. Perry and I will be free to publish it ourselves now."

"That's good. And your dissertation?"

"Should have it done by spring."

"It's Dr. Tyson after that, eh? Your buddy Officer 23 will really love you then."

"I doubt he'll much care, where he is now," Paul replied.

"Yeah, working security in that gated community. Downstate somewhere, right?"

"Kalamazoo."

"And what exactly was he fired for?"

"He got caught soliciting a bribe to reduce a traffic violation charge. The driver of the vehicle was a judge's daughter, and she nailed him."

"Good for her," said Joan.

"Yeah," said Paul. "By the way, I heard the other day from Dave Washington that the autopsies of Jake and Arty revealed their blood alcohol at three times the legal limit. How did they even find the dock that day?"

"Well, at least they missed us."

"Neither was wearing a seatbelt, and both died instantly of head injuries."

"Like poor Ron, only quicker. How ironic and how sad."

Paul nodded. "And it's hard to shake the feeling that they all died because of me."

"Look. Ron was in that hold because he was hiding your notebooks, and the hatch hit him by accident. Those two jerks were after you from the very beginning, thanks to Officer 23's stupid stunt. It was all very sad, as I said, but you shouldn't have any regrets about your own involvement."

Paul raised his eyebrows. "Well, I certainly do have regrets about losing control of my temper, which got me in jail, indicted, and crosswise with you."

"True. But you did get control eventually."

"Eventually."

Paul thought some more. "There's another one."

"Another what?"

"Regret."

"What's that?"

"I didn't see Sidewinder Sally at that Beaver Island bar."

Joan drew back her foot to give him a swift kick in the pants, but she was interrupted by a strike on her line that banged her rod down hard on the transom rail. Jerking back the big rod, she hooked, fought, and landed a twenty-five pound steelhead trout. It was odd to be disappointed in catching that magnificent fish, but Joan wanted only Coho. Lucky for the steelhead, it was released, flashing deeply into the blue water. Just as she recast, Paul got a huge strike on his own line.

"Wonder what the lab people are doing this afternoon?" said Joan.

"Don't know, don't care," replied Paul as he set the hook, braced his feet on the transom and played the big fish.

# AUTHOR'S NOTE

The idea for this novel appeared and developed over many of the years of my career as a freshwater and marine biologist, and some of the dialogue and action are composites of things I heard, saw, or did as a student and a professional in the aquatic sciences. However, the characters in the story are all fictitious, including the nefarious "Officer 23" and the prosecutor, neither of whom to my knowledge resemble anyone present or past in the criminal justice system in Grand Traverse County.

The university and limnology institute in this story are also fictitious, and although I set their location in the approximate area actually occupied by the Great Lakes Campus of Northwestern Michigan College, including the Great Lakes Maritime Academy and the Great Lakes Water Studies Institute, I have never been affiliated with those institutions and did not use them or their personnel as models for my story in any way.

The lighthouse and keeper's bungalow on St. Helena Island are real, and are described in this book as they were in the late 1950s when I visited there as a teenager while assisting my father and his colleague on a Lake Michigan geology cruise. The lighthouse facility has long since been renovated and restored, and now serves as a site for Great Lakes heritage workshops held by the Great Lakes Lighthouse Keeper's Association.

The book's research vessel, *Halcyon,* is a fictitious sister ship of the vessel operated in the 1960s and 70s by the University of Michigan as RV *Inland Seas,* shown in the cover photo taken by Steve Schneider, to whom I am grateful for providing it to me. *Halcyon* was actually the name of a smaller commercial fishing boat chartered for research by the U of M in the 1950s. The hatch cover incident that is center stage in my story is based in reality. I will never forget coming within inches of suffering the same fate as did my character Ron Withers beneath just such a falling hatch while I was working aboard the *Inland Seas* as a student technician on a rough day in Lake Michigan.

As for plagiarism, other than catching a few of my undergraduate students at it in their writing assignments, I have never been personally affected by it. But more than one of my former faculty colleagues have been victims of this unfortunate, dark side of academia.

I am grateful to my friend, author Mary Sanders Smith, for critically editing my first draft and offering many valuable suggestions. Thanks also are due to my former student, Brian Negele, who after his biology degree became an environmental attorney (though not the model for the one in my story). Brian helped me correct several important legal aspects of the story. However, for dramatic purposes I left in a couple of inaccuracies regarding local jurisdiction and Michigan punitive damage law. Helpful edits of later drafts were provided by my cousin Linda Hohm and her husband Chuck, and by my sister Barbara Locke and brother-in-law John Locke (Commander, U.S.N. Retired) who corrected some errors in the nautical material. Thanks to my daughter-in-law Vicki for my author photo.

Finally, I thank my wife, Lynn, who is also a former biologist and oceanographer, for her love, support and companionship throughout my professional career and for her encouragement and final editing of my new adventure into fiction writing.